THE BAKER STREET
IRREGULARS

The Case of the
Missing Masterpiece

TERRANCE DICKS

Blackie

© 1978 Terrance Dicks
First published 1978 by Blackie & Son Limited

ISBN 0 216 90456 0

The Blackie Publishing Group
450 Edgware Road, London W2 1EG
Bishopbriggs, Glasgow G64 2NZ
Set in V.I.P. Bembo by
Western Printing Services Ltd, Bristol
Printed in Great Britain by
Robert MacLehose & Co. Ltd
Printers to the University of Glasgow

Contents

Prologue

As robberies go, this one was dead easy.

First they climbed the wooden fence at the edge of the woods. There were two of them, one big and fat, one small and thin. Just like Laurel and Hardy. The big one gave the little one a leg up, then clambered wheezily after him. They dropped down into the shrubbery, and started creeping towards the big old house. Both men wore masks made from nylon stockings, and the smaller had a knitted woollen hat pulled right down over his ears. He was carrying a long cardboard tube: the kind posters are sold in.

It was very dark in the wooded garden. There were thick black clouds over the moon, and a night wind sighed spookily through the trees. Both men were nervous, and when an owl gave a sudden hoot, the little one nearly fainted with shock. He turned to run, but the big man clamped a hand on his arm, and dragged him on.

They got into the house by one of the windows at the back. There was a burglar alarm of course but it was practically prehistoric. The fat man chuckled, snipped a couple of wires, and that was that.

Sponge-rubber soles squeaking faintly on polished wooden floors, they crept through the darkened lower rooms, up a curved staircase and into the long gallery that ran the length of the first floor. Up to this point the big one had been in charge, but now the little one took over.

The oak-panelled walls of the gallery were filled with pictures, rows and rows of them in heavy gilt frames. Some were landscapes, some were portraits of pompous-looking types in period dress, some were crowded canvases showing tremendous battles by land and sea. Sabre-waving cavalry, charged in the darkness, and cannons belched out clouds of thick black smoke. The little man produced a tiny torch and moved its little circle of light over battles and bigwigs alike, settling at last on a small painting in an obscure corner. The picture was so dark with age it was hard to make out what it showed, but the little man's torch picked out a murky picture of a tumbled pile of stones. Handing the other his torch, the little man produced a thin-bladed knife and began prying the canvas of the picture away from its frame.

He worked very, very slowly and the big man was sweating with nerves by the time the job was over. He kept making urgent *"Hurry-up"* gestures, but the little man ignored them. The canvas came free at last and he rolled it up very carefully and slipped it into the long cardboard tube.

The big man sighed with relief and turned to lead the way out. A hidden door opened in the panelled wall and light streamed into the gallery.

A tall bald-headed man in a dressing gown stood gaping at them. He looked at the two intruders, saw the empty picture frame, realised what was happening. In an astonished voice he said, "Here, you can't—"

The big man took two very quick steps forward, whipped out a cosh and hit him hard on the head. The bald man's legs buckled, and he started to fall. The big man caught him before he landed and dragged him through the lighted doorway.

There was a small book-lined library on the other

8

side of the door. The big man dumped the body into an armchair, took cords and rag from his pocket, and set to work, binding and gagging his victim. The job was finished very quickly, and the big man hurried from the room.

All this time the smaller man had been looking on from the doorway. As the big man pushed past him, the little man came further into the room. Tugging his hat nervously down over his ears he stood looking down worriedly at the bald man. The prisoner's eyes were open now, there was blood on his forehead and he seemed to be choking. Desperate spluttering noises came from behing the gag. Suddenly the little man snatched the gag from his mouth and whispered, "Don't make any noise till we're gone!" He turned and ran from the room. The big man was waiting impatiently at the end of the gallery.

The two thieves got out the same way they'd come in, through the window, across the garden and over the fence. As they ran towards their car, the thin man was clutching the cardboard tube, full of a kind of guilty pride. It had all been *his* idea, and now they'd actually done it. The contents of that tube were worth a hundred thousand pounds.

1 Challenge

Up to now it was just a story in the papers to Dan Robinson and his friends. Then everything changed.

Imagine the playground of an ordinary London school on a sunny Spring afternoon. The kind of afternoon when there are a million better things to do than hang about in school. The playground was full of excited kids, shouting, fighting, dashing about, all fizzing like shaken-up Coke bottles. Naturally enough: it was the last few minutes of the last period of the last day before half term, and any minute now they were all going to be away from there like bionic rockets.

So what were they all waiting for? The famous fire drill, the last bit of torture school inflicted on you before it had to let you go.

In the middle of all this racket a boy sat quietly reading, head buried in *The Hound of the Baskervilles*. This was typical of Dan Robinson, who never acted quite like anyone else. He'd discovered Sherlock Holmes, and gone completely potty about him. Right now Dan wasn't really in that playground at all. He was with Sherlock Holmes and Doctor Watson on Dartmoor, just as the enormous hound sprang at them out of the fog, with burning eyes and ghastly glowing jaws ... Holmes and Watson fired together—and the book was snatched from Dan's hand.

He looked up. "All right, Webb," he said wearily. "You've had your childish fun. Let's have it back."

11

Pete Webb was Dan's best enemy, a big beefy type who liked to push people about. He invariably scored the winning goal in football—if he wasn't sent off first for foul play. He left a trail of bruised shins at hockey, and he was a murderous fast bowler. He was pretty dim at school work, mostly because he couldn't be bothered to try.

Dan Robinson was about as opposite as you can get. Webb always had to be the centre of an admiring crowd. Dan had one or two good friends, but he was content to be on his own if they weren't around. He was tall and on the skinny side, stronger than he looked, preferred solo sports like tennis, judo and swimming. He was good at subjects that interested him, and bright enough to scrape by in those that he didn't.

Most people got on all right with Dan, though there was a mild feeling he was somehow a bit different. In fact, people who didn't like Webb tended to prefer Dan—in a way they'd become leaders of two rival groups. This bothered Webb more than it did Dan. Webb liked people to be friends with him or frightened of him, and Dan was neither. He just ignored him. This really needled Webb, and he did his best to annoy Dan whenever he could. This business with the book was typical. Webb had been pushing for real trouble all term, and Dan knew that sooner or later he was going to have to fight him. He wasn't looking forward to it, but he wasn't dodging it either.

Dan got up, held out his hand. "Come on, hand it over." Webb jumped back out of reach. "Sherlock Holmes," he read out jeeringly. "It's rubbish, this stuff."

Dan said quietly, "Sherlock Holmes is the most famous detective character *ever*. Those stories have been fantastically popular with millions of people all over the world for about ninety years. Still, don't let it worry you, Webby. I dare say they're all wrong and you're right." He reached for the book.

Webb snatched it away again, scowling. "Still rubbish, isn't it. My dad says detective stories are a waste of time." Webb's dad was in the property business. He thought *anything* that didn't show an immediate cash profit was a waste of time. "I mean it's nothing to do with real life, is it? Nobody could really *do* all that stuff—knowing all about someone just by looking at them."

"Conan Doyle based the character on a Professor he knew when he was a medical student. This Professor often used to tell what people's jobs were *and* what was wrong with them—just by looking at them."

Drawn by the promising quarrel a little crowd was gathering. As usual, there were supporters on both sides. Dan saw Liz and Jeff, his two best friends drifting up, and Webb's mates were gathering too. Webb himself was beginning to feel that, as usual, he was losing the argument. "Well it's not how they solve crimes today is it?" he insisted. "Like on *Z-cars*, or *The Sweeney*."

One of Webb's supporters said helpfully. "Or on *Starsky and Hutch*!" "Or Kojak!" chimed in someone else.

"Who loves ya baby?" someone shouted, and a scuffle broke out.

Dan felt the argument was getting off the point, but couldn't resist defending his hero. "All right, things are bound to change in a hundred years. But Sherlock Holmes' methods were based on logic, and that hasn't changed."

Webb saw his chance. "Oh yeah? Do you reckon *you* could solve a crime today with Sherlock Holmes' methods? A real–live crime? Well, come on, Sherlock, could you or couldn't you?"

Dan felt he'd been trapped, but he couldn't back down. "Of course I could."

"Then what about this robbery at Old Park?" said Webb triumphantly. "Let's see you get that missing picture back!"

"All right, I will. Anything to shut you up. . . ."

Webb gaped at him. Somehow things had gone all wrong. Instead of showing Dan up, he was being shown up himself. "When?" he demanded.

"End of the holiday soon enough for you?" asked Dan calmly. "*Now* can I have my book back?"

A chuckle went round the group. Webb stood there seething. This was the spring half–term holiday. Only a week long, but by the time they all got back to school, everything would be forgotten. And meanwhile *he* was standing here feeling stupid, and Dan Robinson was looking at him with that infuriating grin of his, holding his hand out for the book. Furious, Webb tossed the book carelessly to one side and walked off. The book landed smack in a puddle.

Dan went very white. He picked up the book and tried to brush off the mud. "You're a moron, Webb," he yelled. "You're a stupid, cretinous spastic stinking twit!"

Everything went very quiet. You didn't talk to Peter Webb like that. Webb swung round. "Say that again."

"Which bit?" asked Dan. "Moron? After that it went stupid, cretinous . . ." Webb rushed at him, but Dan was ready. He'd expected the rush, in fact he'd deliberately provoked it. He was full of a calm,

14

detached anger, watching his own actions as though they belonged to someone else. As Webb came hurtling towards him, Dan grabbed him by right sleeve and left lapel. He yanked him sideways so all Webb's weight was on his right foot. Dan's own right leg swung forward and back, and swept Webb's right leg from under him, and Webb flew up in the air and landed flat on his back with a thump that knocked the breath out of him. For a moment Webb lay there, shocked and gasping. He scrambled to his feet, fists doubled—and a voice said, "Oy!"

Potty Benton had appeared on the school steps. Potty was the English master, a tall thin character with a shock of wild grey hair. He'd got his nickname not because people thought he was mad, though quite a few boys (and staff) thought just that, but because years ago he'd once shouted to a dullish class, "Show some life, blast you let's see some *enthusiasm*. You look as if you were all sitting there on your potties." Potty Benton he'd been ever since.

The little group drew back warily. You never knew with old Potty. Nice as pie sometimes, but when he lost his temper. . .

"What's going on here?" bellowed Potty.

"Just a little friendly discussion, sir," said Dan quickly.

"*Discussion*? That no doubt is why Webb was flat on his back just now?"

"Well, it was more of a practical demonstration sir. We were arguing about whether boxing was better than judo, and I was just showing Webb the basic *O-soto-gari*."

"Don't gabble your Japanese jargon at me, boy!" roared Potty. "If it wasn't the last day of term I'd . . ." The jangle of the fire alarm came from the school.

"Saved by the bell," said Potty grimly. "Save your *demonstrations* for the gym in future, Robinson. Now hoppit!"

A stocky fair-haired boy shoved his way through the crowd and handed Dan his book. This was Jeff Webster, Dan's best friend. "Here you are, it's not too bad. I got most of the mud off the cover."

Dan nodded his thanks, picked up his briefcase, and put the mud-stained book away. They made their way across the playground where the usual chaos was building up, as windswept teachers, tried to gather their classes around them, yelled at them to kindly shut up and started to call the register, fighting against the noise created by every other teacher in the school doing exactly the same thing

"You were saved by the bell all right," said Jeff cheerfully. "You'd have had no chance to use your fiendish oriental tricks a second time. Webby's twice your weight. He'd have clobbered you."

"Don't be too sure," said Dan. But he knew Jeff was right. Judo in the gym was one thing, but in a serious playground fight its uses were limited.

"You should have taken up Kung-Fu," said Jeff cheerfully. He mimed a wild Kung-Fu kick, and nearly fell over.

They found Mr. Spenlove, their class teacher and joined the straggling line in front of him. The fire drill dragged on. There was the usual idiot in the toilet who'd failed to hear the bell, and had to be hauled out by an angry teacher—to the usual cries of "Don't go sir, don't risk your precious life in those roaring flames!" On their return teacher and boy were greeted by wild applause and calls of "Three cheers for our gallant fireman!"

It ended at last, the headmaster made a brief and

inaudible speech and they were *free*. Jeff and Dan started drifting towards the gates.

"Not a bad throw, that," said a cool voice. "Your footwork was a bit off, though." Dan's other best friend had joined them—a thin, fair-haired girl called Liz Spencer. "He's a right male chauvinist pig, that Webb." Liz was a keen supporter of Women's Lib. She was a tough, wiry girl, who had dealt out many a thick ear as a practical demonstration of her principles.

Dan grinned. "I didn't hear Webb complaining."

"You will—any moment now," said Jeff.

They'd reached the main gate, and Webb stood waiting for them with a knot of his friends. Dan ignored him and kept strolling steadily forward. Jeff doubled his fists—and so did Liz. As they came level, Webb called, "Hey Robbo, I still owe you something."

"That's right, so you do. A new copy of *The Hound of the Baskervilles*."

Webb was deflated once again. Confrontations with Dan never went quite the way he planned them. He took an angry step forward, fists doubled. "That's not what I—"

A piercing toot from across the road interrupted him. Webb's mother had just drawn up in the family Mercedes. The Webbs had recently moved to a bigger and posher house some way from the school, and most days Webb was collected and delivered by car. Webb hesitated, and his mother tooted again. She was a sharp-tongued lady who hated to be kept waiting. He turned to cross the road. "I'll be looking for you next term, Robinson."

"It doesn't have to be a new copy," said Dan helpfully. "Second hand will do. Try the bookshops in Charing Cross Road!"

"I'll get you your book, all right—*when* you solve

the Old Park Robbery!" Pleased with this parting shot, Webb ran across the road and disappeared into the big black car.

As it roared away, Jeff nudged Dan in the ribs. "Saved by the toot, that time. This really is your lucky day!"

Dan was gazing after the car, apparently lost in thought.

"Don't worry," said Liz consolingly, as they began walking down the hill. "He'll have forgotten all about it next term."

"Old Webby?" said Jeff, cheerful as ever. "Never. He'll spend the holiday training, lifting weights to build up those mighty muscles. Soaking his fists in brine, like the old-time prize fighters. I'd enjoy the holiday if I were you, Dan. It'll probably be your last!"

"I won't let him forget," said Dan suddenly. They all stared at him. "You heard what he said. He'll get me a new book when I solve the Old Park Robbery. Well—I'm going to solve it."

2 Background to a robbery

There was a moment's astonished silence. Then Jeff said, "Come on, Dan drop it. Just because old Webb needled you ..."

"Anyway, the police will get the painting back any day now," said Liz hastily. She had the strangest feeling Dan was serious.

Dan said, "It's been over a week, and they still haven't got anywhere. Not according to the papers."

"Well, there you are," said Jeff. "If they can't manage it, how can you?"

"I can give it all my attention," said Dan. "The police have got hundreds of crimes to worry about, new ones cropping up every day. Since that painting was stolen there've been two bank raids, a payroll snatch, a West End jeweller's robbed and a big fraud case in the City. The police are under-manned to start with. How much time can they give to just one crime?"

"You tell them, Robinson," piped a voice from somewhere around knee level. "We can do it!"

Everyone groaned. Even without looking, they knew it was Mickey Mouse. In his usual uncanny fashion, he'd crept up on them without anyone seeing. Sure enough it was Michael Denning, known to everyone in the school as Mickey Mouse. He was a few years younger than the rest of them, and small for his age at that. Not really a member of their group, but a sort of licensed hanger-on. Mickey Denning was a small bony boy, all knees and elbows. He had a thin, sharp face, close-cropped hair, and two enormous ears that stuck straight out from his head—which accounted for his nickname. But into that tiny body was packed the energy of a whirlwind and the soul of a hero. Mickey had the cheek of the devil and he was afraid of nothing. He was youngest of an enormous Cockney family. Youngest and smallest, Mickey had soon learned to stick up for himself. He was a born fighter.

They didn't even bother telling him to go away. It would have been a waste of time. Mickey's cheek had earned him many a clip on the ear from bigger boys, Webb most of all, and he had appointed himself Dan's keenest supporter. When Mickey decided he was in on something, he stuck like glue.

Liz gave Dan a pitying look. "Do be sensible Dan," she said in her most grown-up voice. "People our age don't go round solving crimes. Not even in your old Sherlock Holmes stories."

"That's just where you're wrong! What about the Baker Street Irregulars?"

"The how much?" said Liz. She wasn't a Sherlock Holmes fan.

"They were a gang of ordinary London kids," explained Dan. "Street Arabs they called them. They used to make enquiries for Sherlock Holmes, follow people and stuff like that. Sherlock Holmes said they could go anywhere and do anything. No-one took any notice of them because they were only kids. Well, it's the same with us, isn't it?"

Mickey was jumping up and down with excitement. "Of course it is! Aren't we brighter than any grown-up? Don't we see more and know more than any of 'em realise? Don't they ignore us and shove us around just because we're young? This is a chance to show what we can do." Liz and Jeff looked at each other. It was a difficult appeal to ignore—especially since they agreed with it. "Well..." said Liz slowly. "We could try..."

Jeff, always the cautious one, tried a final objection. "These kids in your book, they didn't do it by themselves, did they? They had Sherlock Homes to help them."

Dan grinned. "You don't need Sherlock Holmes," he said. "You've got me!"

Jeff gave him a friendly shove. "Robinson's Irregulars, eh? Conceited idiot."

"We need a name though," said Mickey.

"How about the Magnificent Three and a half?" said Jeff.

"Or the Frightful Four?" suggested Liz.

Dan ignored the teasing. "Look it doesn't matter what we call ourselves. But I'm going up to Old Park House as soon as it opens tomorrow. Anyone who wants to is welcome to come with me."

"Why don't we go now?" said Mickey impatiently.

"Because," said Dan solemnly. "I must first compile my notes upon the case. My investigation begins tomorrow, ten o'clock, at the scene of the crime." With that, he waved and went off.

"I'll be there," shrieked Micky, and dashed across the road to go down *his* turning.

Jeff looked at Liz. "Couple of idiots. You going?"

"I might," said Liz casually. "If I've nothing better to do. What about you?"

"Depends. I mean, we often go to Old Park anyway..."

Suddenly they burst out laughing. They were both going to be there and they knew it.

"Your mum home?" asked Jeff.

Liz shrugged. "Don't know." Liz's mother was a freelance journalist, and worked long and irregular hours. Liz and her older sister were used to looking after themselves.

"Want to come home for tea? Mum won't mind. She likes feeding you up."

Liz hesitated. Jeff's mum was *always* home. She was a plump, placid woman who wore an apron most of the time, and spent her life in a steady round of dusting, polishing and cooking for Jeff, his dad, and his two brothers. According to Liz's viewpoint, she was an exploited slave. Worse still, she seemed to like it. Liz saw Jeff giving her a teasing look well aware what she was thinking. "I hope you're not expecting me to sell my principles for bread and jam," she said severely.

"Not just bread and jam. Cake! She was making a jam sponge when I came out this morning. *And* some scones."

Liz sighed. Jeff's mum's jam sponge was worth going a long way for. And the scones... Liz sighed. "All right, thanks. At least I can see you male chauvinists don't pig the lot!"

Mickey's family lived in a terraced house close to the Market, which was very handy since most of them worked there. He put his fingers through the letterbox and pulled out the key which hung on a long string behind the door. The key was usually on the string at Mickey's house. The place was crammed with people all going in and out at different times, and if you gave them their own keys they always seemed to lose them. Simpler to leave the key on the string. Up till midnight, anyway. Then Mickey's dad performed the ritual of locking up, and anyone who came in after that was in trouble. Mickey's dad was a great one for the good old-fashioned ways.

Mickey went down the passage and into the back kitchen where his mother was peeling potatoes, his sister was perming her hair, his older brother was cleaning a bike-wheel, and his other older brother was building an Airfix model. No-one took any notice of him and he went straight to the bread-bin and sawed himself a huge doorstep of bread from the loaf and started spreading it with jam.

His mother said, "Get off that, you'll spoil your tea," and aimed a clip at his ear, Mickey dodged it, and went on spreading. Clips on the ear were a form of communication in his house. "And don't go sloping off tonight, your dad wants you to help him load the van."

Mickey nodded absently. He had every intention of sloping off, and his mum knew it. It was simpler to agree than to argue. There was always plenty of work flying about in Mickey's house—the trick was to keep out of its way.

Mickey grabbed his *Monster Fun Comic* from under a chair and wandered off reading and munching. He went into the middle room and curled up on the sofa. (The front room was sacred, used only for weddings, funerals and Christmas.)

Mickey tried to get on with his comic but somehow the *Creature Teacher* and *Terror TV* didn't hold his attention. He kept thinking about the next day. Imagine solving a *real* crime. That'd make his family sit up and take notice. Mickey felt like the invisible man sometimes. It wasn't that he was actually neglected, or that anyone was unkind to him. But with so many large and noisy people rushing about, he sometimes felt lost in the crowd.

He wondered how old Robinson got on. Must be funny, being an only child. . . .

Dan stuck his finger on the doorbell and leaned and after a bit his mother appeared, with a ball point pen in her hand and an accusing look on her face. "You're early."

"Half-term," said Dan patiently. He'd told her that morning, he'd told her every morning that week, he'd known she'd forget and she had.

He gave her a peck on the cheek and slipped past her, and she followed into the long room that took up all the ground floor of the house. It had originally been two rooms but they'd had it knocked through to make an open-plan living and eating area. Mrs. Robinson had a little office area in one corner. She scratched her head with the ball-point, leaving a blue mark on her forehead.

"I was just trying to draw up the agenda for tonight's meeting. The Council people are being very difficult about the Townsend Road project. . ."

Dan's mother was a part-time social worker. At least she was supposed to be part-time. She spent her days in a whirl of meetings, discussions, seminars and committees. Each committee seemed to spawn several more, all terribly important, and somehow she just got busier and busier. Dan's father, an architect who'd just set up his own firm was equally busy and often had to go abroad on business trips—he was off on one now. With all this going on, the family didn't often see very much of each other.

Dan knew his parents had originally planned on three or even four children, but somehow they'd just got too busy, and he'd ended up as an only child. So, what with one thing and another, Dan spent a good deal of time on his own, at least when he was at home. Not that he was complaining. He was used to it, and on the whole he quite liked it.

While his mother rattled on about her problems, Dan went over to the bread-bin, cut himself two slices of bread, buttered and jammed them, made some orange squash and put the whole lot on a tray.

Meanwhile his mother was saying, "The trouble is darling, they've called an emergency committee meeting of the housing committee tonight and I really must go, so I'll be popping out any minute now. Still I think I've just got time to get you something to—"

Balancing the tray on one hand Don opened the door, gave his mother another kiss on the cheek and disappeared up the stairs. "... eat," concluded his mother, as the door closed behind him. She stood frowning for a moment, and then went back to her desk.

Dan's room was at the top of the tall old house, right under the roof. It was long and thin with a sloping roof, and since he didn't have to share it with anyone he'd made it into a kind of bed-sitter, with separate areas for all his different activities.

When his mother had bought a bigger desk, Dan had bagged the old one, so he even had his own office. He perched the tray on the desk-corner, took out a notebook and a biro and began compiling a proper dossier on the case he had so rashly promised to solve. Where should he start?

Start with the facts, he decided. He went down into the sitting room below and began rooting through the pile of old newspapers on the sofa, thankful, for once, for the fact that his mother never had time to throw anything away. He dug out the local paper, with the story of the robbery and several daily and evening papers for the following days and carried them up to his room. He went through the papers one by one, cutting out the various accounts of the robbery, and arranged them in order in a cardboard folder. He began by studying the first account of the robbery in the local paper.

DARING ART ROBBERY screamed the headlines. MYSTERY MASTERPIECE STOLEN. The Gazette didn't often get a major *local* crime story, and it was making the most of this one.

Munching thoughtfully on his bread and jam, Dan read and re-read the newspaper stories, extracting solid facts from excited journalistic prose. The facts were few enough.

The picture had been stolen from a collection of paintings in the local not-so-stately home: Old Park House. The place had been built by some nineteenth-century tycoon, who'd got his knighthood and settled down to live the life of a gent, in what was then a little village on the outskirts of London. Over the years the town had crept up and swallowed the countryside, but somehow the house and its huge gardens had managed to survive. But as times changed the descendants of the original tycoon had found it harder and harder to keep the place going. Just after the war the present heir had followed the example of the owners of far more stately homes, and opened the place to the public.

Mind you, Old Park House was a long way from Woburn Abbey. It was a nineteenth-century copy of an eighteenth-century mansion, very nice to look at but with no real historical value. It housed a jumbled collection of nineteenth-century art and sculpture, most of it pretty awful. Old Sir Jasper Ryde had bought his paintings by the yard, and the dealers of the time had taken him for a pretty good ride. . . . The house was full of the most awful Victorian junk—busts and statues, huge paintings, over-stuffed furniture and ghastly ornaments of every kind. Over the years some of this stuff had acquired a certain value. Yesterday's junk is tomorrow's antiques. But there had been nothing very special about, until the picture restorers had called—and found a painting by Constable hidden amongst all the junk. The painting was another version of Constable's *Stonehenge*, a sort of early practise picture.

Obviously some dealer of the time had bought it cheap, not realising its value himself, and palmed it off on Sir Jasper mixed up in a load of the usual rubbish. And there is had stayed, hanging in a dark corner of Old Park House all these years . . . until the man from the picture cleaners turned up, spotted it, and declared it to be *not* a copy but a genuine early Constable, worth at least a hundred thousand pounds.

Obviously what the present Sir Jasper *ought* to have done was whipped the thing straight off to a bank vault. But apparently he'd planned to feature it on special display, to attract more visitors, before putting it up for sale. Meanwhile, he'd failed to do anything about his rather elementary security set-up. Two days, or rather two nights after the picture had been discovered, a couple of villains had walked into the house, hit him over the head, and walked off with the picture. Now, well over a week later, the police still hadn't been able to find any trace of it. Or if they had they were keeping quiet about it. The story had gradually become smaller and smaller in the national press, fading away completely by the weekend. This week's Gazette had only a small back page paragraph, saying investigations were proceeding and the police expected important developments soon—whatever that was supposed to mean. Probably nothing very much, thought Dan. There was also an appeal for anyone with information to contact the local CID.

He pushed aside his dossier and slumped into his old armchair. Definitely what Sherlock Holmes would have called a three pipe problem. But Dan didn't smoke, and a three-gobstopper problem didn't have the same ring to it. Still, there was something else Holmes used to do to help him think. Dan lugged his violin-case from under his bed and took out the violin. He began scraping away at the violin, trying to produce those 'sonorous and melancholy chords' with which Sherlock Holmes used to madden Doctor Watson.

The sound of the violin floated down through the house. In the kitchen, Dan's mother looked up in surprise. Dan usually had to be nagged into violin practice. She went back to her work, little realising that just above her the Great Detective was grappling with his very first case.

The fat man pushed his way through the door of the little pub by the market and took a quick look round. It was just on opening time. The bar was cool and dark, and almost empty. From the corner, a voice said, "Over here, Eddie." Another man was sitting at a corner table, a pint mug of bitter and a glass of lager on the table before him. He was a stocky broad-shouldered man, smartly dressed in a grey suit and grey hat. The fat man drained half the bitter in one swig. "How did you get on, up West, then?"

The other man took a sip of his lager-and-lime. "Got a few nibbles. But it's very slow."

"Look, it's been over a week now," whispered the fat man.

"Takes time, Eddie, takes time. Not flogging a case of dodgy watches are we? Or a few cans of beans fell off the back of a lorry? You've got right out of your class this time." He lowered his voice. "We're talking in *thousands*. That takes *time*."

"What about that Sheik then? Or that Yank? Thought they were dead keen."

"They are, both of 'em. Soon as one of 'em meets my price, we're away."

The fat man took another swig of beer. "Why wasn't the perishing thing insured? . . . " He sounded almost indignant.

"Well, it wasn't. So—we've got to find a buyer." The stocky man's voice was quiet and definite. It was obvious who was in charge. After a moment he said, "What about Sammy?"

"What about him? Only going about sweating great drops, isn't he?" said the fat man contemptuously. "Turns his coat collar up every time he sees the Law."

"You reckon he'd talk? If they pulled him in?"

"Just as soon as they asked him!"

The stocky man nodded thoughtfully. "We may have to put him away then."

"You're not talking about . . . " the fat man's voice tailed off.

"Not necessarily. But suppose I was? He's served his purpose, we don't need him any more." The stocky man emptied his glass and shoved it towards the other. "Your round, Eddie."

As he carried the glasses to the bar, the fat man was sweating. Sometimes his brother frightened him.

3 The scene of the crime

When Dan arrived at the gates of the gardens sur-
rounding Old Park House he found Mickey waiting
for him. He was wearing his school satchel, and from it
he produced a very large magnifying glass and a tin of
talcum powder. Dan pointed to the magnifying glass.
"Where'd you get *that?*"

"Pinched it from my brother. He collects stamps."

"What's the talcum powder for?"

"Fingerprints! They always dust for prints."

"Put it away. They won't let you sprinkle talc over
the paintings. Anyway, we wouldn't know what to do
with a fingerprint if we found one."

Mickey put his equipment away, clearly hurt at
Dan's lack of appreciation.

Jeff arrived next, strolling casually up as if he just
happened to be passing. "I'm not taking any of this
seriously you understand. But it's a nice day for a
walk."

Liz came running down the path to join them. "It's
ten o'clock *exactly,*" she announced. "I don't want any
cracks about women always being late—you're all
early!"

"As if we would," said Jeff. "Well, get a move on,
you're late!" He dodged Liz's punch and they started
walking up to the house.

It was a sunny spring morning and as they walked
through the woods it struck Dan that they might easily
have been coming here anyway. Old Park was a

favourite haunt of theirs. Admission to the grounds was free, though you had to pay to get into the house itself. Somehow, the fact that the place was so run-down made it all the more attractive. There were dense woods where you could disappear without trace, an overgrown lake where you could swim and fish, straggling lawns for improvised games of football and cricket. Best of all, there were *no* notices saying no this and no that, and *no* park keepers to tell you off. There was one crabby old gardener but if you kept away from his flower beds he left you alone. There was even a cafe in what had once been the coach-house, a cool stone-floored room decorated with horses-brasses and bits of old coaching equipment.

They were the first arrivals and the old lady at the admission desk was still settling herself in when they arrived in the hall, but she hunted out her cash-box and sold them three half-price admission tickets—10p each.

Dan led the way up the curved marble staircase to the picture gallery. They walked across the long, echo-ing room, and grouped themselves in front of the blank space on the wall in the far right-hand corner. "Well, there it is," said Liz. "Or rather there it isn't!"

Jeff nodded. "The scene of the crime. Well, don't just stand there, Sherlock. Detect something!"

Dan knew they were only teasing, but his heart sank all the same. He saw Mickey looking expectantly up at him, talcum powder and magnifying glass at the ready. His confidence in Dan's powers was even worse than the others' mockery.

Dan felt the difference between real life and books come rushing in on him. It was all right for Sherlock Holmes. He usually arrived on the scene of the crime pretty promptly. Words written on the wall in blood,

31

nice fresh footprints in the mud, exotic cigar stubbs left about—something to work on. Here there was *nothing*. Just a light patch of unfaded wall where the picture had once hung. Even Sherlock Holmes wouldn't have been able to make anything of that.

Or would he? Just as in the playground the day before, Dan found part of his mind seemed to have started working by itself.

"For a start," he heard himself saying, "They knew just what they were looking for. It was almost the smallest picture in the gallery, and the only really valuable one." Dan gestured towards one of the enormous battle scenes. "I mean, they'd have had a much bigger job getting one like that away and it probably isn't worth the effort."

"I'm afraid you're all too right," said a sad voice behind them. "A dealer offered me ten pounds—and he said *that* was for the frame!"

An oak-panelled door had opened in the oak panelled wall of the gallery, and a man stood looking at them. He was tall, and thin, he wore a baggy brown tweed suit, and there was a strip of sticking plaster across his balding forehead. Dan knew at once who it was—he'd been looking at his picture in the Gazette only yesterday. This was Sir Jasper Ryde—owner of Old Park House and ex-owner of the stolen painting.

Sir Jasper was a shy bird as a rule, and only rarely popped out of his living quarters in the private part of the house. But he was always terrifically polite to any visitors he encountered, treating them as if they were private guests he'd bumped into by chance.

He smiled rather shyly at the little group. "I was surprised to hear voices out here so early. But I gather your interest is in crime rather than in art?"

They all gave embarrassed grins. Jeff began shuffling away, and the others followed. All except Dan. His heart was pounding, but he forced himself to speak up. "I know this sounds daft. In fact it probably *is* daft—but we were thinking about investigating this crime. It was a sort of bet..."

Sir Jasper stared at him in astonishment, and Dan struggled on, "I expect you're sick of the whole business by now. But if you *could* spare a minute or two to talk about it..."

Sir Jasper's long, sad face had broken into a smile. "Boy detectives eh? Like the Famous Five and the Secret Seven?"

"Boy and *girl* detectives" said Liz firmly.

"We were thinking on the lines of the Baker Street Irregulars," said Dan.

Sir Jasper was delighted. "You're a devotee of the Master then? Splendid!" He looked at Jeff's stocky figure. "This is your Watson, I take it? Then he looked down at Mickey, who was gazing up at him in speechless astonishment. "And this is..."

"He's the Irregular," said, Dan thinking Mickey was about as irregular as you could get.

Sir Jasper looked apologetically at Liz. "I'm afraid there's very little place for women in the Sherlock Holmes stories. There's always Mrs. Hudson, the faithful housekeeper..."

"Forget it" said Liz firmly.

"What about Irene Adler?" suggested Dan. He grinned at Liz. "She was a sort of international adventuress—very liberated. One of the few people who ever got the better of Sherlock Holmes."

"That sounds more like it," said Liz.

"And to Holmes she was always *the* woman," said Sir Jasper delightedly. "Yes, Irene Adler by all means." He turned to Dan. "And now my dear Sherlock, I shall be happy to assist your investigations in any way I can. Shall we go into my study?"

Dan knew it was all a bit silly, but he couldn't help feeling pleased as he followed their host through the door. Jeff was thinking it was lucky the old boy had turned out to be another Sherlock Holmes nut, Liz was making up her mind to read the story with Irene Adler in as soon as possible, and Mickey was still speechless at the calm and confident way in which Dan was chatting up the aristocracy.

The library was a book-lined room with sagging leather armchairs, and even more sagging sofa, and a scattering of chairs and tables. There were almost as many books on the floor and on the chairs as on the shelves. Sir Jasper shifted a few piles to make room for them, and said, "Sherry? No, perhaps not, too early. I could make some coffee?"

"Nothing thank you," said Dan firmly. He didn't want to waste a minute of this precious questioning time.

Sir Jasper was deep in thought. "I've always believed Watson was wounded in the *left* leg," he announced suddenly. "Though mind you, there is a very good case to be made for the right." He looked hopefully at Dan, obviously expecting a nice juicy discussion on Holmseian scholarship. Dan refused to join in. "The left, I'm sure," he said. "Now about the robbery, Sir Jasper."

"Call me Jim," urged their host. "Silly name Jasper, always hated it. Family name you see, got stuck with it. Terrible time at school and in the Army. That song, you know."

Dan knew he was being sidetracked, but he couldn't help asking, "Song?"

Jeff grinned. "It's easy to see you're not a rugby

34

player. What you do is, you sing, 'Oh, Sir Jasper do not touch me' over and over leaving off one word each time. So it goes, 'Oh, Sir Jasper, do not touch, Oh, Sir Jasper do not, Oh, Sir Jasper do. Oh, Sir Jasper, Oh, Sir, Oh!' "

Sir Jasper, the real Sir Jasper, glanced meaningly at Liz and coughed reprovingly. Jeff blushed and muttered, "Well, it's all pretty harmless really." Liz muttered something about childish male chauvinists, and Dan made a desperate attempt to get the conversation back on the subject.

"Now about this robbery," he began again. He couldn't decide whether he was being invited to call Sir Jasper 'Jim' or 'Sir Jim' and decided to leave it out altogether.

Sir Jasper sat upright and said solemnly, "I am all attention"—and Dan found he couldn't think of anything sensible to ask.

A sudden inspiration came to his rescue. "Since we're right here on the spot why don't we reconstruct the crime instead of just talking about it?"

Sir Jasper, who was very keen on amateur theatricals, jumped up enthusiastically, and immediately took charge. "That's the idea. You all go outside and pretend to be stealing the painting. I'll be sitting here reading, just as I was on the actual night."

He bustled them out into the gallery, where by now a few early-bird tourists were wandering about. They all looked in mild surprise as the four children came through the door.

"What do we do now?" whispered Jeff.

"You heard him," said Dan cheerfully. "Steal the painting. You and Mickey can be the robbers."

Jeff nodded towards the curious tourists. "They're all *looking*."

"Ignore them. Come on get on with it! Liz and I will observe."

Jeff made a few awkward gestures towards the blank space on the wall.

"Put some *go* in it," said Liz unkindly. "You're stealing a painting, not washing the windows!"

Jeff made vague cutting motions, and Mickey jumped up and down making great slashing sweeps that would have had the painting in shreds. The curious tourists started edging closer, and Jeff went scarlet with embarrassment.

There was worse to come. The door to the study was flung open, and Sir Jasper appeared shouting, "Aha, you scoundrels, caught in the act!"

Dan thought it was time to intervene. "Did you actually say that?"

"Well, no" confessed Sir Jasper. "I think I probably said something brilliant like 'Er...'"

"And what did you *see*? Was that anything like it? What these two were doing."

"No. The small one was at the painting, and the big one was holding the torch."

Dan shoved Jeff and Mickey into position. "Like that?"

"More or less. The one cutting seemed to be working very carefully."

Mickey did his imaginary cutting with finicky precision.

Dan nodded. "What happened then?"

"The big one hit me on the head," said Sir Jasper sadly.

"What with?"

Gingerly, Sir Jasper touched the plaster on his forehead. "You know I'm not really sure..."

"Was it hard, like an iron bar? Or soft, like a rubber truncheon?"

"I know it sounds silly, but I don't think it was either. It was hard and flexible, at the same time."

"Couldn't have been something like, oh, a canvas sausage packed with sand?"

Sir Jasper nodded. "Yes, that may well have been it."

Dan looked at Jeff. "All right, get on with it. Cosh him."

Jeff shot him a murderous look, stepped up to Sir Jasper and aimed a feeble blow at his head. To his horror, Sir Jasper immediately fell down, giving a realistic groan.

The tourists gasped in astonishment. A Japanese couple clapped politely and took several photographs.

"Now what?" asked Dan.

From the floor Sir Jasper said, "You drag me through into the library."

With a little help from their victim, Jeff and Mickey dragged him into the library. They closed the door behind them, much to the disappointment of the tourists, who were waiting for the next bit of the show.

Following his instructions they bundled him into a chair and mimed the tying up and gagging, Jeff very sketchily, Mickey with great enthusiasm. Sir Jasper told of the tightness of the gag, and the way the smaller robber had taken it out. He suddenly became very serious as the reality of that night came back to him. "The gag was very tight. I think I would probably have choked if he hadn't taken it out."

"Let's just go back to that," said Dan. "Mickey, you mime taking the gag out."

As Mickey obeyed, Dan leaned over Sir Jasper. "Imagine it's all happening again. Try to see the men again. Is there anything you can remember. Anything else at all? How were they dressed for instance?"

"Dark clothes," said Sir Jasper, struggling to remember. "They wore masks. Oh yes, and the one who helped me was worried about his hat. He was wearing one of those woollen caps sailors sometimes wear. He kept fiddling with it, pulling it down to meet his mask."

"Anything else? His voice? His hands?"

"The voice was just ordinary, not educated but not specially rough either." Sir Jasper glanced at Mickey's grimy little hands just under his nose. "There *was* something about his hands though... He had to take his gloves off to get the gag out. His hands were very white... and there was something else... a smell..."

Suddenly Dan shoved Mickey out of the way. "Jeff, let him smell *your* hands."

Puzzled Jeff obeyed, and Sir Jasper said, "Yes, that's it. That's it exactly."

Jeff drew his hands back guiltily, and Dan stood up. "I think that's all for now. Can I come back if I think of anything else?"

"Yes, of course." Sir Jasper seemed almost disappointed the demonstration was ended. "It would be marvellous if you *could* find it," he said. "Between you and me, I don't think the police are very optimistic. And it wasn't insured, you see. I didn't have time to insure it, I'd only just discovered it was valuable. I was relying on selling it to save the old place."

"Save it?" asked Liz. "Save it from what?"

"Being sold. Torn down for flats and offices."

Liz was horrified. "You wouldn't let them do that, surely?"

"I might have to. It's an old house, and it's in very poor condition. If the roof gets much worse the council might even condemn it. It would cost thousands to get the place repaired and I just haven't got the money."

The Irregulars looked at each other in horror. Old Park House had been part of their lives for as long as they could remember, and they suddenly realised how much they would miss it.

"You see, the house may be falling down but the site itself is very valuable," explained Sir Jasper. "I've had several very attractive offers—but the thing is, I *like* the old place. All I really want is to go on living here."

"We like it too," said Dan quietly. "And I promise you we'll do our very best to help."

The coach house cafe was open by now, and they held a conference over doughnuts and coca-cola. They were all in a much more serious mood. Solving the mystery had been a kind of exciting game up till now—the realisation that Old Park itself was in danger had made it all much more important—and more worthwhile.

Jeff took a swig of coca-cola and stifled a burp. He looked expectantly at Dan. "All right, mastermind, this is where you amaze us with a stream of brilliant deductions I suppose?"

"All right," said Dan obligingly. "The crime was carried out by two men who were fairly recent acquaintances. One is a professional criminal with several convictions for robbery with violence, the other has no previous convictions, a fairly junior job in the antiques business, and a very nervous disposition." Dan looked round at their astonished faces. "Oh yes, and one more thing. The smaller of the criminals had bright red hair!"

4 Cops and robbers

Dan couldn't help enjoying the way Liz, Jeff and Mickey sat staring at him in pop-eyed astonishment.

Then Jeff burst out laughing. "And I suppose the other one had an Irish grandmother and has recently returned from Afghanistan?"

Liz looked hard at Dan. "You're serious, aren't you?"

Dan smiled. "Well, more or less. I don't say it's all cast-iron, there's too little evidence. But the deductions are all reasonable"

"All right, Sherlock," said Jeff grimly. "Now suppose you just explain where you got all that."

Dan took a deep breath. "We know there were two of them, right? Now—look at the way they acted. One keeps calm as anything, thumps Sir Jim and gags him, and clears off with the loot. He didn't hesitate to use violence, he was carrying some kind of special cosh—*and* he didn't care if the poor old boy choked or not. Came all ready with the tape and the gag, and the cosh. Someone like that's bound to have previous convictions."

"What about the other one?" asked Liz. "How do you know they'd only just met?"

"Because the little one was so nervous. And look at the way he acted. He even worried about the victim choking. If the professional one had *known* he was like that he'd never have risked doing the job with him."

Jeff still wasn't really convinced, though he couldn't

find any real flaws in Dan's logic. "Okay, so far so good. Now, what about the job in the antique trade?"

"Well, why was the little one there at all? Because he knew about the painting, where it was and what it looked like. He took the painting from the frame. He was the art expert. So, there's at least a chance he's in the business. That's where your hands come in, Jeff."

Jeff sniffed his hands defensively. "I still can't smell anything."

"That's because you're too used to it. You were helping your dad decorate last night, right?"

Jeff nodded. His dad was a fanatical do-it-yourselfer, and treated home decoration like the men who paint the Forth Bridge. As soon as he came to the end, he started again at the beginning. Jeff's mum had the smartest house for miles around. She also had to live with the perpetual smell of paint and—"Turpentine," said Jeff. "He could smell turpentine where I cleared the paint off my hands."

"That's right. That stuff clings for ages, even after you wash. Now, I reckon the chap we're looking for probably works with his hands picture framing, furniture restoring things like that. He got that painting out of its frame neatly enough."

Suddenly Mickey piped up. "Tell 'em about the red hair." He spoke as if *he* already knew the answer, and just wanted it explained to the others.

"Well, you remember what Sir Jasper said, about him always fiddling with his hat. He was more worried about hiding his hair than his face. Now, what colour hair do people *always* remember?" Dan looked round. "Dark like mine, fair like Liz, brown like you Jeff, or mouse like Mickey, no one really notices. But *red* hair stands out like a lighthouse."

Jeff was still looking hard for an objection. "Suppose he was *bald?*"

'I thought of that," said Dan seriously. "But he had very white hands remember. Red hair and white skin often go together."

Jeff sucked the last of his coke up the straw with a satisfying gurgle.

"It's all like—candy-floss. Airy fairy! All spun out of nothing."

"Nothing's all I had to start with."

"But there could be a hundred other explanations for all those things you guessed."

"All right. Name one, just one, that's *more* likely than what I've suggested."

Jeff thought hard. He couldn't.

"All right," said Liz. "So now we know a little bit about the criminals. What do we do now?"

Dan stood up. "We do what people in detective stories never do—we go to the police!"

"You're barmy," said Jeff. "They'll never listen to you."

"I don't suppose they will," agreed Dan. "But if we try, and they don't take any notice—no-one can blame us for going ahead on our own..."

The police station was an ancient building in the High Street, tacked on the even more ancient town hall. It was built from that peculiar kind of red stone that seems reserved for public buildings.

Dan went up the stone steps and into the reception area. (The others had refused to come with him, and he'd agreed to meet them later).

He found himself facing a wooden counter, behind which were a lot of olive green filing cabinets, and two shirt-sleeved policemen drinking tea. They looked different somehow and Dan realised it was because they were without their helmets. One of the policemen came forward shoving a big open ledger along the counter. "All right, son, what is it? Lost dog? Lost purse?" There was a heard-it-all before tone in his voice.

"Neither. I've got some information about the Old Park House Robbery."

The policeman nodded, unimpressed. "Let's have it then."

"It says in the paper to inform CID."

"You tell me, and if I think it's worth it, I'll tell them."

This didn't suit Dan at all. "I'd sooner tell them myself," he said calmly. "Then *they* can decide if it's worth anything."

The policeman leaned threateningly over the counter. "Look, son, I don't want any cheek."

"Nobody's giving you any cheek. I'd like to talk to someone from CID please. If there's no-one there, tell me when there will be and I'll come back."

There was a nasty pause. Dan could see that this particular policeman was just the kind of adult he couldn't bear—the kind who thinks nothing any one under twenty-one says can possibly be of any importance. Talking to him would be a waste of time.

A voice behind him said, "What's up then?" Dan turned and saw that a young man in a very smart suit and a rather flashy tie had followed him into the station. He had thin, sharp features, and a vaguely raffish look—like the people who sell things out of suitcases on the pavement.

The policeman gave a rather malicious smile. "Customer for you, Happy. Knows something about the Old Park job—too important to tell me."

The young man looked hard at Dan and said, "That right, kid?" His voice was sharp, but not unfriendly. Dan just nodded.

"Come on, then. This way." He led Dan through a side door, along a short corridor, and into a tiny office, which was almost completely filled with a desk, a chair, and two green filing cabinets. "Here we are," said the young man cheerfully. "The nerve-centre of local crime-detection. A mini Scotland Yard." He sat down behind the cluttered desk. "Detective-Constable Day at your service." He waved Dan to a chair and fished a pencil stub and notebook from the pile of papers. "Name? Address?" Dan told him. He scribbled quickly then said, "All right, let's have it."

His tone was calm and businesslike, completely serious, and Dan decided that here was someone he *could* talk to. "It's all a bit complicated,,' he said. "It may sound silly at first. Will you just let me tell it straight through? If you think I'm wasting your time you can just sling me out." The young man nodded without speaking and Dan launched into his story. As briefly as possible he told of his visit to Old Park, the meeting with Sir Jasper, and the series of deductions he'd made about the crime. It all sounded pretty thin, as he was talking. As Jeff had said, it was a bit like candy floss.

When he'd finished the young policeman nodded briskly and said in a rather surprised voice. "You know that's not bad. Not bad at all. We missed that bit about the smell of turps. All theory, though, isn't it? Especially the red hair."

"You'll follow it up though?"

Detective-Constable Day shook his head. "Can't. Nothing to do with me any more. I'm not on the case."

"Who is then?"

"My esteemed superior Detective-Sergeant Summers is on the case," said Day, with more than a tinge of bitterness in his voice. "Various distinguished detectives from Scotland Yard are on the case. But not me. I've got other things to occupy my time." He tapped the bulging folders on his desk. "You know what's in these? The phantom flasher down at the recreation ground. An outbreak of knicker-nicking on the council estate. Pavement-fouling by certain canine criminals. An epidemic of fruit pilfering down the market... That's the sort of big time crime they give *me* to deal with."

Dan grinned sympathetically. Clearly Day was a very junior detective, and was being treated like one.

"But you *were* on it—in the beginning?" he asked.

Day nodded. "On the preliminary enquiries, sure. Then the big boys took over. *They* think it was one of the big London art gangs."

"And you don't?"

"No. Wasn't insured, was it? The big boys would have made sure about that."

Dan was puzzled, and he seized the opportunity to improve his criminal know-how. "Do they only pinch things that are insured?"

"Some things, yes. Take a painting for instance. If it's valuable it can be identified, traced. Who's going to buy it if they can't hang it up? Some mad millionaire with a secret museum? But if it's all nicely insured... Well, there's the customer... ready made."

Suddenly Dan understood. "The insurance company... they pay to get it back?"

"Stands to reason, doesn't it? Say the painting's insured for twenty thousand. It gets nicked and the company are due to fork out the full amount. but if they turn over ten thousand to some go-between, no

45

questions asked—then the painting turns up, they make a saving, and everybody's happy especially the villain who nicked it. But this painting wasn't insured. Someone nicked it on impulse, and now they're stuck for a buyer."

"And you think it's a local job?"

Day went to the filing cabinet and took out a file. "All comes down to knowledge and opportunity, doesn't it. Just like they say in Police College . . . Old Sir Jasper's stony broke, finds he's got a hidden treasure and within a matter of days it gets nicked."

Dan said eagerly, "So how many people knew about the painting? Who knew first, apart from Sir Jasper himself?" He answered his own question. "The man from the picture restoring company!"

"Right. So what do we do? We check him out. Result, nothing. Old established local firm, Rundle and Son, both as straight as a die. No financial problems, just the reverse, they're rolling in it. No chance they'd go bent for a mere hundred thousand. They were due to handle the sale, anyway. They'd have copped a fat commission, and a lot of valuable free advertising."

"They could have talked about the painting, told somebody," said Dan thoughtfully.

"They *could*, in fact they probably did, but they swear they didn't. Result, dead end."

Day looked at his watch. "Look, I can't go to my guv'nor with the kind of stuff you've told me. They'd have me back directing traffic. I can't give you any official encouragement either. Kids aren't supposed to get mixed up in crime. Could be dangerous."

Dan stood up. "Well thanks for listening to me. I won't waste any more of your time."

"That's all right. Makes a change from chasing the dirty dogs."

Dan paused by the door. "I know you're not actually *on* the case—but if you got some sort of tip-off... wouldn't it be your duty to investigate it? Just to see if it was worth the attention of all these important superiors of yours? And if it happened to end up in your getting the painting back, and all the credit, well, no-one could blame you for that, could they?"

Detective-Constable Day looked narrowly at him for a moment. Then he scribbled a number on a scrap of paper and pushed it over. "Can't really tell anyone's age from a voice on the phone," he said absently. "And a tip-off is a tip-off."

Dan grinned, pocketed the paper and headed for the door.

Day bent over the typewriter, and began tapping laboriously at the keyboard.

After a few words he stopped, gazing into space. Funny kid, that, he thought. Dead serious. Talked a lot of sense. Day was still young enough to remember what it was like to be a kid, to live in a world where other people ran things, and all thought they knew better than you did just because they'd lived a bit longer.

He thought about Detective-Sergeant Summers. Come to think of it, things hadn't changed much. He got on with his typing.

5 Rundle & Son

"Yes, I think I can say I've established a working relationship with my colleague in the police," concluded Dan grandly—and ducked, as Liz threw a cushion at him.

The Irregulars were having a conference in Dan's room; he'd just finished telling them about his meeting with Detective-Constable Day.

"What's all this chatting up the cops then?" jeered Mickey. "Thought we were going to do it all ourselves and show them up?"

Jeff said very seriously. "Now listen, all of you. I suppose there is just a chance we'll get on to the thieves. But don't forget, we're dealing with the sort of people who bash other people over the head with coshes. They're liable to turn very nasty at the thought of losing a hundred thousand pounds. If we ever do think we're really on to them, we turn the whole thing over to some nice large coppers." He turned to Dan. "Either that's agreed, or we pack the whole thing in, here and now."

Dan nodded. "Quite right. That's why I made contact with Day. We want someone who'll listen to us when the time comes."

"You really think he will listen?" asked Liz doubtfully.

"He might. He's still young, not that much older than us. I get the feeling no-one pays much attention to him because he's just a beginner in the CID."

"Ah," said Liz sympathetically. "Never mind, when we hand him the case on a plate, they'll probably make him an Inspector straight away!"

Dan said, "I'm glad you're so keen, Liz. The next bit of investigation's up to you?"

"It is?" Liz looked suspicious.

"We need someone to ask questions at Rundle's, that picture restoring place. Now, who else can go around being nosey apart from detectives?" Dan answered his own question. "Journalists, that's what. And who's a leading light on the school magazine?"

"Got you," said Liz, jumping up. "You want me to interview him, and find out who he might have talked to. I'll go over there right away."

"Not like that you won't," said Dan. "Go home and change."

Liz looked at her jeans and T-shirt. "Change? These are clean on."

"Put on a dress," said Dan patiently. "You have *got* a dress, haven't you?"

"Of course I've got a dress! I suppose you'd like me to put a ribbon in my hair, and flutter my eyelashes at the big important businessman?"

Dan patted her on the head. "Now you're getting the idea."

Liz snorted indignantly.

"What about the rest of us?" asked Jeff.

Dan considered. 'I don't think you and I can do much at the moment, not till we get some more leads. There's a job for Mickey, though."

Mickey said eagerly. "About time too. What do I do? Tail someone? Pull 'em in for questioning?"

Dan chose his words carefully. "Don't get me wrong, Mickey, but they're a pretty tough crowd in the market. I imagine your dad and your brothers meet all kinds of people. Ask if they know of anyone who's big and fat—with a record of robbery with violence. . . ."

On her way home, Liz thought things over, and decided Dan was probably right. You had to put on the right act if you wanted grown-ups to take you seriously. She put on a dark blue dress, and brushed her hair till it looked neat and severe. She even fished out the glasses she was supposed to wear for reading, and put them on. Clutching her largest notebook, she made her way to Rundles.

The antique shop was at the top end of the High Street, the posh bit, where all the smarter places were bunched together. Rundles was just a discreet shop-front, with one small painting in the window arranged against velvet drapes. Inside, the shop was cool and dark with soft fitted carpets and an air of restrained luxury.

An elegant young lady came forward to serve Liz, and heard her request to see the owner with polite astonishment. "Ai'm afraid Mr. Rundle is very busy," she purred. "If you could tell me what it's about?"

"I'm afraid not," said Liz, equally sweetly.

"Then ai don't really think it will be possible."

Liz's journalist mother had given her some very practical advice. 'Get your foot in the door, and keep it there! Just keep talking—and never give up!'

So Liz stood her ground. "Will you tell Mr. Rundle I'm here, please. *He* can tell me if he doesn't want to see me."

A door behind the counter opened and a tall white-haired man appeared. Liz seized her opportunity. "Mr. Rundle?"

He frowned down at her in a lordly way. "Yes? What is it? I'm extremely busy."

"I've been sent here by our school magazine. We're doing a feature on the old-established businesses in the district. Just the really *distinguished* ones, of course, the ones with *real* tradition. So naturally we came to you first of all."

Liz was remembering more of her mother's advice. "If anyone's important, or even if they just think they're important, then flattery is what they want, and plenty of it. Lay it on with a shovel."

It worked, too. Mr Rundle glowed visibly at Liz's honeyed words. "Well of course I am very busy, young lady . . . but I'm sure I could spare a moment or two . . . Come this way, please!"

The snooty assistant sniffed, and Liz couldn't resist a triumphant grin.

Mr Rundle's office looked as if he'd kept all the best antiques in the shop for his own use. It was lushly carpeted, there were paintings and sculptures everywhere, and all the furniture looked as if it belonged in a museum. Liz perched on a spindly gold chair and Mr Rundle settled himself behind an enormous leather-topped desk, on which several no doubt priceless antiques were being used as paperweights. He was quite an artistic sight himself, tall and thin with beautifully brushed white hair, and a suit that looked as if it had cost as much as a small Picasso.

Before she could get to the real purpose of her visit, Liz had to go through with the pretend one. She was a good interviewer, and did a conscientous job. Mr. Rundle happily told her about the number of years his firm had been established, the many valuable works of art they'd handled, their very important clients. He told here about his young son Peter, just down from Oxford, who was going to take over the business, and keep up the family tradition. At last Liz was able to work the subject round to picture restoring, and to Mr. Rundle's visit to Old Park House. "It was really very clever of you," she said, "spotting a masterpiece amongst all those worthless old paintings. I bet you rushed round telling everyone all about it."

"I did no such thing," said Rundle severely. "Discretion is the most important part of a business like mine. I told *no-one*—except Sir Jasper of course. He asked me to put the picture on the market. Tragically, the painting was stolen before I could do any more about it."

Mention of the stolen painting seemed to make him rather uncomfortable, and after a few more questions he stood up as if to end the interview. A tall fair-haired young man came into the office. The family resemblance was obvious. He was a younger but equally elegant version of Mr. Rundle himself.

"You must be Peter Rundle," said Liz quickly. "We were just talking about the painting your father discovered. The one that got stolen so soon afterwards."

Peter Rundle stared at her. "What *about* the wretched painting?" he said sharply. "Father, who is this?"

Mr. Rundle explained about Liz's interview, and Peter Rundle said petulantly, "Write about the firm by all means, I'm sure father's told you *all* about *that*. But for heaven's sake keep off that wretched painting. It's caused us nothing but trouble. The number of times we've been over it all with the police. I mean, it's not my fault if the old fool didn't look after it. Father told him what it was worth."

Mr. Rundle took Liz by the arm and opened the door. "Our young friend doesn't want to bothered with all this, Peter. Goodbye, my dear. Be sure to send me a copy of your school magazine." A few minutes later, Liz found herself out on the pavement, blinking in the sunlight of the busy high street.

Thoughtfully she made her way down the hill, hardly seeing the bustling shoppers. She was pretty sure she'd discovered something. The only thing was, she wasn't quite sure what!

Liz went round to Dan's house early that evening and found him alone in the big kitchen frying sausages and heating baked beans. "You live like a hermit in this place," she accused. "Don't you mind?"

Dan jabbed a sizzling sausage with a fork. "No, I like it. Means nobody bothers me."

"Where's your mother?"

"Down at the Town Hall. Housing committee meeting or something. Where's yours?"

"Covering the same meeting for the local news agency!"

"There you are then," said Dan. "Keeps 'em out of mischief, I suppose. Stay for supper? I can chuck in some more sausages, and there's plenty of beans."

Over the meal Dan listened keenly to Liz's account of her visit to Rundles. He made her go over it several times, concentrating not so much on *what* had been said, but the *way* it had been said, and on her impressions of Peter Rundle and his father. Finally he said dramatically, "Qui s'excuse—s'accuse!"

"What's that?"

"Who excuses himself, accuses himself. It's a quotation from some eminent frog."

"I know what it means," said Liz witheringly. "What I mean is what do you mean . . . if you see what I mean."

"Just about. Now listen. As soon as you mention the painting young Peter gets all ratty and says it wasn't his fault it was stolen—which means it very likely *was* his fault."

"You think they're behind it?" Liz found it difficult to think of the elegant Mr. Rundle as a secret master-criminal.

"It's possible—but I doubt it." Dan was thinking aloud as he carried the plates to the sink and took a packet of ice-cream from the fridge. "I mean if Rundle wasn't honest, he needn't have told old Jasper the painting was worth thousands in the first place. He could have bought it for fifty quid and Jasper would have jumped at it. I think Rundle senior's probably too snobbish to be a crook. Wouldn't risk getting his name in the vulgar newspapers. No, it's the son and heir who interests me. He was the one who really reacted."

"Maybe he's desperate for money," suggested Liz. "Gambling debts, or something. Slow horses and fast women!"

"I suppose it's possible. But he doesn't sound like much of a raver. I imagine if he got into any trouble he'd go running to daddy, and daddy would fork out the necessary."

Liz was getting annoyed. "Well, what do you suspect him of?"

Dan finished his ice cream and pushed the bowl aside. "It all comes down to *information*. Who knew the painting was valuable?"

"The Rundles."

"Right. And if they didn't steal it, they must have talked to someone."

"Not according to Mr. Rundle. And they told the police the same thing."

"Well, they would, wouldn't they?" said Dan. "People always lie to the police, if they think it will get them out of trouble. Just think, Liz. Old Rundle spots a really valuable painting in a collection of junk. According to you, he's a pompous old twit to start with. He must have been full of himself. And who's the first person he'd tell?"

"Son Peter, the apple of his eye!"

"Right. And suppose *Peter* boasts about it to someone else who tells someone else... Some local villain finally picks up the story and pinches the painting. We need to check up on young Peter's contacts and trace the link."

"Dan, are you really sure about all this?"

Dan scratched his head. "I don't know really. It all seems to make sense, doesn't it? There just wasn't *time* for the information to reach some big-time crook, it all happened too quick. Remember what Day said—experienced art-thieves would have made sure the painting was insured. But one of our robbers was a professional all right. Think of the burglar alarm, the way he thumped Sir Jasper and tied him up."

"And the little one?" asked Liz. "The one you say had red hair?"

Dan frowned in concentration. "Suppose *he* was the contact man—the one who picked up the information. He told the real crook—who took *him* along to identify the picture."

Liz waved her ice-cream spoon. "Theory, my dear Holmes all theory. How do we find these theoretical villains of yours?"

"Elementary, my dear Watson. We leave it to our smallest Irregular. That famous secret agent, known to the underworld as Mickey Mouse!"

6 Mickey's mission

"Dad, do you know any villains?"

Mickey's father was at the kitchen sink, shaving the tricky bit under his nose. He put down the razor, rinsed and dried his face, and said vaguely, "What's that, son?"

"Villains, Dad. Proper crooks."

Mr. Denning looked down at his youngest son in mild astonishment, as if he was surprised to see him there at all. Mickey was used to this reaction. He was the youngest of his family by at least five years, having been as Mr. Denning put it, 'A bit of an afterthought.' In a house full of strapping teenagers, he tended to get overlooked. Not that his parents didn't love him as much as their other children. They just forgot he was there a lot of the time.

"Villains," said Mr. Denning thoughtfully. He began unscrewing his razor, cleaning it, drying it, and returning it to its case on the shelf over the sink.

Mrs. Denning watched from the ironing board and said, as she did every night, "I don't see why you can't shave in the bathroom."

Mr. Denning replied, as *he* did every night. "I *like* shaving in the kitchen. My dad *always* shaved in the kitchen. Had one of the old cut-throat razors he did. Used to sharpen it on a leather strop. Warmed my backside with that strop many a time..."

Mickey felt like screaming. He'd heard all this at least a million times. Sometimes he thought his parents were like giant waxworks, with tape recorders inside, trundling round the same paths, doing and saying the same things day after day. "Villains, Dad," he shouted. "Crooks! Do you know any?"

Mr. Denning took his freshly ironed shirt from his wife and started putting it on. "None of these collar-attached shirts when I was a lad. Separate white collars it was, held on with studs. My mum used to scrub 'em—*and* starch 'em."

Mr. Denning became aware that for some reason his youngest son was jumping up and down and tugging at his trouser leg. "All right, son, all right. Now what was it? Do I know any villains." Mr. Denning considered. "Well, not so as to say 'Morning Fred, how's the burgling going' to any one. Or 'Nice bit of break-ing and entering last night, was that you?'"

Mickey groaned. That was the trouble with grown ups, If they weren't going on about the rotten good old days they were making terrible jokes. You never got a straight answer from them. "Please Dad, it's *important.*"

"Why? What do you want to know about such things for?"

Mickey was taken aback. "It's just something we're doing Dad," he said vaguely. Then he had a sudden inspiration. "It's a kind of *project.*" This last word did the trick. Mr. Denning was well aware that schools these days had given up *proper* education (which meant sitting in rows chanting your multiplication tables) for something called projects, which involved asking a lot of daft questions, and sometimes actually going out and looking at things.

Mrs. Denning recognised the word as well. "Stop tormenting the boy, and tell him what he wants to know. It's for his school."

Mickey kept a pair of fingers crossed behind his back. He hadn't actually *said* it was for school. If people liked to jump to conclusions...

Mr. Denning frowned, as he struggled to explain the facts of real life to his youngest son. "Thing is son, it's not all clear cut, like on the telly. Goodies and baddies, and stuff like that. Like there might be one or two people I might have my suspicions of. People who are unexpectedly flush now and again, buying drinks all round, or chucking it away in the betting shop. Blokes who occasionally disappear for a while and come back with a very short hair-cut. Blokes who might offer you a watch or a telly or hi-fi very cheap because it fell off the back of a lorry. Now, some people might call those people villains. Difficult to prove it, though—and unhealthy to go asking questions. I don't bother them, and they don't bother me."

Nobody actually bothered Mr. Denning very much. He was six foot four and bulky with it, he had fists like hams and muscles like an ox, from humping crates about, and he had six sons as big as he was, or getting that way. (Not including Mickey of course.)

Mickey scratched his head. It was all turning out more complicated than he'd bargained for. He tried to remember what Dan had told him to ask. "Do you know any *fat* villains, Dad. Fat, *nasty* ones?"

Roy, Mickey's oldest brother had come down from the bathroom and was listening to the conversation with interest. "There's Big Jock," he suggested. "They sent him away for a stretch for doing a bank. He's still inside though."

A few more bulky villains were discussed but none of them seemed to be exactly what Mickey wanted. It was Mrs. Denning who said, "What about that Fat Eddie Simmonds. He was always a nasty piece of work. Coshed that old lady postmistress he did, nearly killed her."

"Be fair," said Mr. Denning judiciously. "He's more of a retired villain. Been going straight since they let him out. His brother Harry stood by him. Gave him a job down his scrap yard."

They chatted about the Simmonds brothers for a while longer, producing between them a quantity of information that would have done credit to the files at Scotland Yard. It appeared that Eddie had always been the 'bad' one, getting into steadily more serious trouble, while his brother, who had a spotless record, waited for him to come out of prison, always ready with help and a job to go to.

Mr. Denning put on his coat, and kissed his wife. "Might as well step out for a quick one," he said—as he did every night. "Night, Mickey, you be good. See you later, Mother, shan't be long." Mr. Denning and Roy went out.

Two of Mickey's sisters came in and started discussing their dates for the evening in very unflattering terms. Mickey said goodnight to his mother and slipped away to the room he shared with two elder brothers. They were both out, so he had it to himself.

He sat hunched up on his bed, hands round his knees. He was shivering with excitement. Surely this was what Dan wanted. A local villain, big and fat, and nasty enough to cosh old ladies. Mickey knew what he *ought* to do—wait till the morning and report his discoveries to Dan. But also he knew what he was *going* to do. He was going to take a look at Simmonds Yard—tonight!

Half an hour later, Mickey climbed out of his bedroom window, down the drainpipe, on the the scullery roof, and into the yard.

He was wearing black jeans, black plimsolls and an old black sweater. In his bed was a dummy made from his pyjamas, blankets pulled right over it. His brothers were used to finding him asleep when they came up to bed. Chances were they'd assume the huddled shape was Mickey, without even looking at it. He let himself out of the back gate and ran silently up the alley behind the house.

Simmonds Yard took quite a bit of finding. It was in an area of shabby warehouses, obscure little factories and trading estates that fringed the banks of the canal. The canal was more or less disused now, though some local people had formed a society to keep it open. There was a little marina in the main canal basin, where people kept cabin cruisers and lovingly-restored longboats.

The yard turned out to be the end of a little blind alley just next to some abandoned warehouses. Two big wooden gates ran right across the end of the alley. They were closed and locked, and there were spikes on top. The green-painted gates were weathered and peeling, and someone had painted 'Simmonds Yard. Strictly Private' across them in straggling white letters.

Mickey thought hard. The front gate didn't seem a good idea. Too high, and too exposed—anyone seen coming down the alley was obviously making for the yard gates. Better try round the back.

Behind Simmonds Yard was an empty warehouse, and that wasn't nearly so well defended. Mickey climbed a sagging wooden fence, crossed a yard littered with rusty oil drums and found himself up against another barrier. Between the warehouse grounds and Simmonds Yard was a high wire-mesh fence, with two strands of wire running across the top. White letters on a red notice-board read 'Danger—Electric Fence' A skull-and-crossbones was daubed underneath.

For a moment Mickey felt like packing it in. It was getting dark now, and Simmonds Yard looked spooky and threatening in the gathering dusk. It was a big sprawling place, just an area of wasteland really, dotted with mountains made from the bodies of dead cars. Rust stained the weed-grown ground like blood, and maimed cars stood dotted about like survivors from some ghastly mechanical war.

Mickey had his heroes too, though James Bond was more in his line than Sherlock Holmes. He thought of his hero breaking into Goldfinger's secret hideout. Mickey wished *he* was six foot tall, with a Walther PPK and an Aston-Martin with built-in machine-guns and an ejection seat for unwanted passengers. On the other hand, he thought it was highly unlikely that Simmonds Yard would be guarded by a giant oriental assassin with a steel bowler hat—let alone hordes of Chinese killers and an old granny with a tommy-gun.

Considerably cheered by this thought, Mickey began looking for a way in. He followed the fence to the corner, where it made a right-angled turn. It was pretty clear the fence ran all the way round the yard. It would be tricky to climb—too spindly to give much of a grip, and there was no way to avoid getting caught by the electrified wire on the top.

Mickey followed the fence round looking for a possible weak spot, and at last he found one. On one side of the yard a patch of waste ground, bordered the high fence. Ground, not concrete. Bare earth. Micky hunted round till he found a flat stone and started to dig. There are advantages in being all skin and bone. It didn't take long to scoop a hole under the bottom of the fence, and as soon as it was deep enough he wiggled through.

Once inside he ran to the cover of a pile of rusting cars and considered his next move. Now he was inside, he wasn't sure what he was going to do. Presumably there would be some kind of office near the front gate. Dodging from hiding-place to hiding-place like a commando Mickey began working his way across the yard. Luckily the heaps of wrecked cars and piles of metallic scrap gave plenty of cover.

The office was there all right, a sagging wooden hut just inside the high front gate. As he got closer, Mickey was thrilled to see light shining from the windows. Maybe the crooks were having a meeting. Perhaps he could eavesdrop, and learn their secret plans. Maybe they'd be kind enough to mention where they'd hidden the painting. He could get it back, stroll casually into Dan's house with it tucked under his arm.

The office hut was in an area of open ground, and Mickey knew he'd have to risk going right up to it if he was going to be able to hear anything. He dropped to the ground and covered the distance in a fast commando crawl—he hadn't watched all those old war movies on telly for nothing. Now he was one of the attacking British Commandos at the beginning of *Rommel—the Desert Fox*.

Mickey dropped down at the back of the hut, and put his ear to the wooden wall. He could hear movement, scraping sounds, and the low mumble of voices but he couldn't make out any words. He'd have to get under a window, or even creep near the door. . . .

He was working his way along the back of the hut when a great black shape padded up out of the darkness, giving him the fright of his life. It had fierce red eyes, a lolling tongue, and rows of great gleaming teeth. It was the biggest dog he'd ever seen in his life. Big as the Hound of the Baskervilles, he thought fleetingly. Bigger.

The dog gave a low rumbling growl, and its teeth closed on his arm.

7 Captured!

Mickey kept perfectly still. He was good with dogs and knew a lot about them, and one of the things he knew is that they don't like sudden panicky movements. He noticed that although the dog's teeth had clamped down on his arm, the pressure was just enough to hold him, and no more. He'd read somewhere that some dogs could carry an egg about without breaking it. He hoped very much that this dog was one of them.

Soothingly he said, "All right, boy, I'll keep still." The dog looked solemnly at him, and released his arm. Mickey started to edge away. The dog gave a low warning growl, Mickey sat still again. Raising its head the dog let out a series of deep, booming barks. Mickey couldn't help admiring the dog's intelligence. It had caught its prisoner, and now it was sending for help.

He heard a door open, and a man came running round the side of the hut. He was big and bulky, and he looked like an angry gorilla in the dusk. "Well done, Killer," he rumbled. He grabbed Mickey by the arm and dragged him round the building and into the little hut.

Scared as he was, Mickey still remembered to take a good look round. He was here in the villain's lair, and anything he saw might turn out to be a vital clue. Trouble was there wasn't too much to see.

The hut was a simple wooden building like the kind you see used as an office on building sites. It held a

battered table a few rickety chairs, an old roll-top desk
and a sagging brown armchair with the stuffing coming out. The only touch of decoration was a new-
looking poster showing different sorts of British birds,
tacked up on the wall behind the desk. The place was lit
by a single electric light-bulb dangling from the ceil-
ing. It was a long way from the secret underground
hideout of Doctor No—but Mickey was determined
to stay cool, just like James Bond. Not that these two
were likely to stand him a slap-up meal. The only sign
of food was a half-eaten pork pie on the desk.

Mickey turned his attention to the two men. The
one who'd caught him was big and fat with a round
face. He was sweating, as if even the little run around
the hut had been too much for him. He wore a
shabby blue suit, and a grimy white shirt open at
the neck.

The man in the archair was very different. He was
broad-shouldered and stocky and he wore a neat grey
suit, with a matching light-grey shirt and silver-grey
tie, and well-polished black shoes. His face was just a
face, completely ordinary. Except for the eyes. They
were the same silver grey as his tie, and utterly, icy
cold. He looked casually at Mickey and said, "What
have you got there then?"

"Kid, innit?" said the fat man, "Killer caught him.
Told you the dog was a good idea."

The grey man turned to Mickey, "What you doing
in our yard, son?" he asked softly.

"Playing," said Mickey. He tried to sound calm, but
somehow his voice came out a frightened squeak.

"Other places to play, aren't there?" said the grey
man reasonably. "Parks and playgrounds and that.
Yard's private. Saw the notice didn't you? How did
you get in?"

Mickey said nothing and the fat man grabbed his ear and twisted it. "Answer the man, sonny."

"Yes, I can read," he said. "It was just a bit of fun that's all," said Mickey desperately. "I found a gap under the fence and wriggled through. I was playing commandos."

The man in the chair shook his head. "Mad about war, these kids. What are we going to do with him, eh, Eddie?"

"Why don't we chuck him up on the electric wire?" suggested the fat man gloatingly. "Fry like a crisp, he would."

He peered down into Mickey's face for signs of terror. He was clearly the type who enjoyed frightening people.

Mickey *was* frightened, but he was getting angry too, and somehow the anger was chasing out the fear. "Cobblers," he said. He wasn't sure what it meant but it was one of his Dad's favourite words. "I don't suppose that fence is even electrified. And if it was you wouldn't be allowed to make the current strong enough to kill anybody."

"Oh no?" said the fat man feebly. He seemed astonished by Mickey's defiance as if he wasn't used to people standing up to him. "Well, suppose we set Killer on you? Eat you up in a couple of mouthfuls!"

Mickey looked at the dog. It certainly looked hungry enough. For all its huge size it was thin and gaunt, as if they didn't feed it properly. But something told him it wasn't really vicious. "Don't be daft," he said scornfully. "That's a trained guard dog. They teach them to capture people, not to eat them." He patted the big head and said, "Sit!" in a firm voice. The dog sat.

The man in the chair seemed amused. "Tough kid," he said almost approvingly. "Doesn't scare easily." He stood up. "You don't want to pay any attention to my brother, he's only joking." He put a hand on Mickey's shoulder. "*But I'm not*. It really is dangerous in the yard. That's why we have the fence and the notices. Take those piles of old cars. One of them could collapse and fall on you. Or you could climb in an old fridge, get trapped and suffocate. All sorts of ways you could get hurt, even killed. I mean we'd all be very sorry, but it wouldn't be our fault would it? Not if you were poking about where you'd no right to be."

His voice was calm and reasonable and he might just have been delivering a friendly warning. But his hand tightened cruelly on the boy's bony shoulder as he spoke, and Mickey knew he was hearing not a warning but a threat. If the man decided he was dangerous, some kind of accident *would* happen to him—because this man would make it happen. The grey man's quiet words were more terrifying than his brother's extravagant threats. Suddenly Mickey began to feel really scared.

There was a sudden knocking at the front gate of the yard. The fat man looked at his brother. "That'll be him."

"Then let him in," said the other man patiently. He was still looking thoughtfully at Mickey, as if deciding whether to let him go or arrange for that accident after all.

Mickey decided not to wait for a decision. As the fat man opened the gate he wrenched his skinny shoulder from the grey man's grip and sprinted for the gap. He streaked through it like a rocket, bounced off the man waiting outside, nearly knocking his cap off, and tore off up the alleyway.

The dog bounded up to follow, but the grey man cuffed it and shouted "Down!" A huge dog chasing a boy through the streets would bring just the sort of publicity he wanted to avoid.

The fat man pulled their visitor through the gate, and shoved him towards the hut. He turned to his brother. "Want me to go after the kid? I could take the car."

Harry Simmonds thought for a moment, and shook his head. "Forget it, Eddie we gave him a good scare. He won't be back." He turned towards their visitor, a spindly little man in a grimy raincoat with the collar turned up, and an oversized cap pulled down over his eyes. "Hullo Sammy," he said softly. "Me and Eddie have been worried about you."

The little man said nervously. "Worried, Harry? No need for that."

Harry Simmonds smiled coldly. "We hear your nerves have been playing you up. So we're going to help you."

The man called Sammy looked at the grey man, then at his brother Eddie, who was closing and locking the front gate. He wished he'd never agreed to come to the yard, but it was too late now. There was no escape. "Help?" he said nervously. "How do you mean?"

The fat man crept up behind him like some great ogre and whispered hoarsely, "We're going to take you for a little ride."

Mickey swarmed up the drainpipe, climbed into the bedroom window and jumped straight into bed without even taking off his plimsolls. He lay there for a long time, waiting for his heart to stop pounding.

His ear hurt, his shoulder hurt, but his heart was ablaze with triumph. He'd been in the villains' headquarters. He'd got a good look at both of them. He'd talked back to them, just like James Bond, and, again like James Bond he'd pulled off a daring escape. And at the very last moment he'd stumbled on the biggest clue of all.

In the few seconds he'd been entangled with the visitor to Simmonds Yard he'd had time to notice something about him. Under that oversized cap was a head of flaming red hair.

8 Council of war

Next morning Mickey hurried round to Dan's house and told the others about his adventure. He'd expected praise and admiration, but he was in for a disappointment. Jeff delivered a most tremendous telling-off in his best prefect's voice. "We agreed, right at the beginning, we wouldn't do anything stupid, or dangerous. You could have been hurt or even killed, you little twit, and no old painting's worth that."

Liz was just as cross with him, but for very different reasons. "Fancy going off like that, and having all the fun for yourself. This is supposed to be a team you know, we all work together."

It was Dan who came to Mickey's defence. "All right, all right," he said. "I agree, Mickey went too far as usual—but as it happened, it paid off. We've got some really promising suspects now, and some important clues to back up our theories."

"What clues?" scoffed Jeff, changing tack. "He trespasses in an old junk yard and naturally the owners aren't too pleased. They make a few threats to scare him, and let him go."

"They didn't *let* me go," said Mickey indignantly. "I escaped."

"You bunked off, you mean. I suppose if you hadn't you'd have been buried in a nameless grave by now."

"You can't have it both ways, Jeff," Liz pointed out. "Just now you were telling Mickey off for getting into danger. Well, if he was in real danger, he must have been on to something."

"That second bloke was *serious*," said Mickey desperately. "He really would have arranged an accident if it suited him."

Dan made Mickey go over it all again—everything that had happened, everything that had been said, everything he'd seen. He turned to Liz and Jeff. "Let's just suppose Mickey has stumbled on to something. We've got a match for the pair who did the robbery—one fat and nasty one, one small and nervous with red hair. *Hair he's trying to hide with a cap that's too big for him*. The one in grey could be the real boss, the one who planned it all. You've got to admit, it fits a bit too neatly to be pure co-incidence." Dan was pacing about the room in excitement, now his whole face alight with interest. You could almost hear the whirring as his mind worked at double speed.

Jeff looked worriedly at him. To start with it had all been a game, a sort of imaginary crossword puzzle. It had been fun watching old Dan spin his web of deductions, building up a frail structure of theory from a few facts. But now, thanks to that little devil Mickey, Dan's imaginings were becoming solid. Suddenly there was a real place, Simmonds Yard, with real villains who could hurt people.

Jeff was no coward, but he had a very practical nature, and a big streak of caution. He remembered the ugly bruise on Sir Jasper's forehead. It was pure luck the blow hadn't done some real damage.

And if Mickey really *had* stumbled on real villains, it was all too likely that they would have faked an accident if he'd discovered too much—and got away with it too. Reckless kid gets hurt playing on old car dump—happens all the time.

Now Dan was acting as if it was all still a game. Liz and Mickey were just as bad, carried away by the excitement of it all.

Jeff banged his fist on the table. "Now listen you lot, I reckon this has all gone too far. We ought to tell some one. Some adult, or even the police."

Mickey began to protest, but Dan shushed him. He looked at his friend's worried face. "Look Jeff, I know how you feel. I'm no more anxious to get anyone hurt than you are."

"Then go to the police. Or let's tell one of our parents and let them go."

"Tell who? My mum'd never take it in. Dad might listen but he's away on a business trip." Dan hesitated. "Don't get me wrong, Jeff, but do you think it would be any good telling your parents?"

Jeff thought of his mum, her mind full of meals, curtains and getting the washing done. Or his dad, worrying about the dry-rot in the roof, and the inflation in the economy. As far as they were concerned crime was just something that only happened in the newspapers, or on the telly. Jeff nodded slowly. "All right. But there are four of us. What about Mickey's parents. Or Liz's?"

Mickey shook his head. "Dad wouldn't want to know. He always says mind your own business, and keep your nose clean."

"*My* mum might listen," said Liz. "If she thought there was a story in it, she'd be on to Fleet Street in no time."

Dan said, "I think it's too soon for that Liz. We've no real proof, yet. Publicity now would just frighten them off. They could just destroy the painting, and write the whole thing off. Who's going to catch them if they never try to sell it?" He turned back to Jeff. "I'm sorry

Jeff, but I think we've only got two chances. Either we drop the whole thing now, or we go back to the police when we've really got something to tell them. If the Simmonds brothers did steal the painting, no-one seems to suspect them but us. So if we drop it, there's a good chance the painting will never be recovered, and Old Park will have to be sold."

Liz and Mickey both looked anxiously at Jeff. Although Dan was the leader of the Irregulars if anyone was, they couldn't think of going on without old Jeff. Finally he gave a reluctant grin. "All right, we'll carry on for a bit. But remember, everything we do's got to be discussed and agreed by the whole group. No more mad commando raids, Mickey. Agreed?"

Mickey nodded eagerly, so relieved he'd have promised anything. Jeff grabbed the last biscuit. "All right, Sherlock, what's the next move?"

"A bit of observation," said Dan. "We concentrate on finding the link between the Rundles, who knew the painting was valuable and the Simmonds who may have been the ones who stole it. And it's my belief that link has got red hair! So everyone keep an eye out for the redhead Mickey saw. Jeff, you and I will watch the Simmonds yard. Mickey and Liz you've got to keep an eye on the Rundles, and especially on Peter Rundle. Follow him about, and see who he contacts."

There were immediate grumbles from Mickey and Liz, who accused Dan of giving them the boring and safe job while keeping the exciting and dangerous one for himself and Jeff. Dan tried to calm them down. "This is the only possible arrangement. Mickey *can't* go to Simmonds Yard because they'd recognise him from last night. And Liz has *got* to go to Rundle's because she knows Peter Rundle by sight." The logic was a bit shaky, but after a bit more argument, the other half of the team accepted their assignments.

Dan jumped to his feet before they could change their minds. "All right you two, off you go. . . .It's the middle of the morning already." He went to a cupboard and fished out a battered old pair of binoculars without a case.

Liz looked suspiciously at him from the doorway. "The Rundles will already be in their shop, won't they?"

"That's right," chimed in Mickey. "What good will it do us to stand and watch a rotten shop all day?"

Dan had to think quickly. "What about elevenses? Morning coffee and that? That's the sort of time people pop out to meet people. And it'll soon be lunchtime."

Liz gave a sceptical look. "And if Peter Rundle has lunch with someone with red hair, a mask and a rolled up painting under his arm, we'll know we're on to something!"

Dan sighed. "All right, Liz, so it's no more than an outside chance. It was an outside chance when we all went off to Old Park. There's only an outside chance Jeff and me'll see anything at the yard. But one thing's for sure, we won't see anything if we don't go and look!"

Still grumbling Liz went out saying,"All right, all right. Come on Mickey. Women and children last—as usual."

When they'd left the house, Jeff said. "You nearly had a mutiny on your hands there, mate. And Liz was right, wasn't she? You were packing them off on the safe job."

A little guiltily Dan said, "Well, I admit I'm keen to see Simmonds Yard for myself. Young Mickey's done better than any of us so far. He'll be getting big headed!"

Dan fished a war-surplus haversack from under the bed, and led the way down to the kitchen. He handed Jeff a breadknife and a loaf. "Here you are, Watson, get slicing." Dan went to the fridge and looked inside. 'Tin of spam, tomatoes, and good-o, two cans of coke.'

Jeff sawed the crust off the loaf. "What's all this about? Are we going on a picnic?"

Dan started putting food into the haversack. "Detectives are like soldiers, they march on their stomachs. We don't want the villains alerted by the sound of rumbling tums."

Liz and Mickey spent nearly an hour hanging about the High Street, both convinced in advance they were wasting their time. It's not as easy as it sounds, watching a shop. True, a shop isn't exactly going anywhere, but that makes it all the harder.

They didn't want to be seen, so they watched the entrance from the other side of the road, pretending to take an interest in the contents of the shop opposite. It happened to be a furniture shop, about as boring as they come.

"Might at least have beeen a toyshop," grumbled Mickey. He was still grumbling about Jeff and Dan following up his discoveries. To cheer him up Liz sent him off for ice-cream, and they stood glumly licking their cornets looking at the antique shop accross the road. The High Street was busy, and they were jostled by a constant stream of shoppers. Since it was a warm sunny morning, Rundles' door stood open. Liz caught occasional glimpses of the snooty girl moving about behind the counter. Once Mr. Rundle came out from his office, spoke to her for a few minutes, then went back in again. "Big deal," muttered Liz. More waiting. Then Peter Rundle came out from behind the counter. He wore silver-grey slacks, a double breasted blazer and an open necked white shirt with a college scarf at the neck, and looked, thought Liz unkindly, rather like something out of a tailor's window. She nudged Mickey. "There he is!"

Mickey stared at Peter with fascinated interest. "Right old posho, isn't he?"

Peter Rundle chatted for a few minutes with the snooty girl, then came out of the shop and set off down the hill.

"Knocking off for the day!" whispered Mickey. "Dunno how he stands the pace!"

"Stay and watch the shop," said Liz hurriedly. "I'm going after him." Before Mickey could argue she was following Peter Rundle.

The long straggling High Street runs from top to bottom of a sizeable hill, and it gradually changes character as you go down. At the very top are the posher businesses, dress shops that call themselves Couturiers, the expensive hairdressing salons, the jewellers, the fantastically expensive Patisseries that sell real cream cakes, and the art and antique shops—including of course Rundles. Further down you get everyday useful shops, Marks and Spencers, Woolworths and Sainsburys, the newsagents, hardware shops, off-licences. Lower down the hill, things change again. Cafes instead of restaurants, little general stores that never seem to close, old fashioned greengrocers, and fish and chip shops. At the very bottom of the hill is the market. Here in a few narrow streets are crowded an array of colourful stalls selling antiques (or junk), clothes, toys, second-hand books, fish, meat, vegetables, anything and everything that anyone can sell or buy. Liz followed Peter Rundle down the hill and into the market. He made his lordly way through the crowd until he reached a little clothes stall where two girls, one fair and one dark, were looking after a stall full of jeans and denim skirts and dresses. Peter waved at the blonde who said something to her friend, left the stall, and came to join him. He gave her a quick kiss and they went off arm in arm to a crowded cafe on the other side of the road. Liz hesitated for a moment, then followed them in. It was a tiny, crowded place with a counter at the back and a scattering of rickety chairs and tables. Peter and his girl friend managed to find a table for two. Liz perched on a counter stool as near as she could get, and ordered a coffee and a doughnut from one of the two girls behind the counter.

Peter immediately began a long account of how his firm had sold an immensely valuable silver collection to an Arab oil-sheik. He had one of those very penetrating voices and every word could be clearly heard all over the little cafe. Peter's companion *pretended* to be fascinated though Liz saw that she was hiding an occasional yawn. Liz decided the girl really thought Peter a boring twit, but went out with him because he was well off.

Bored with the people she was supposed to be watching, Liz tuned in to the two girls behind the counter, who were chatting in low, urgent voices during a lull in their work. One girl was tall, brown-haired and sharp-faced, the other blonde and plump. The plump one had red, puffy eyes as if she'd been crying a lot recently. The other girl seemed to be consoling her. "Don't worry, Shirl," she was saying. "He'll turn up again. And if he doesn't, he's not worth worrying about is he? Probably got a wife and kids somewhere."

The plump girl burst into tears, and rushed into the little kitchen behind the counter. Liz saw Peter and his girl had finished their coffee and were preparing to leave. Peter tossed some money on the table in a lordly way and strolled out followed by his girl friend. Hurriedly Liz fished out the money for her coffee and doughnut. As the sharp-faced girl took her money, gave her her change Liz said, "Your friend seems very upset."

The girl sniffed. "Her boyfriend's disappeared."

"Gone off and left her you mean?"

"I mean what I say," said the girl fiercely. "Disappeared. They had a date last night and he didn't turn up. She went round to his digs and he wasn't home. She went round this morning before work, found he hadn't been home all night. I reckon he just got fed up with her. The way she's carrying on, you'd think the little ginger twit had been murdered."

9 Trapped!

When they reached the blind alley that led to Simmonds Yard, Dan walked straight past with no more than a casual glance. "Where are we off to?" protested Jeff.

Dan gave him a pitying look. "We're not going to camp out at the gate are we?" He pulled his eyes into slants with his fingertips. "Or wander round disguised as a couple of Japanese scrap metal dealers?"

Jeff said determinedly, "Well, we're not going to break in like Mickey either are we? Not with some great man-eating dog on the loose. So what do we do?"

"Patience, my dear Watson. All will be revealed."

Dan led the way to the abandoned warehouse behind Simmonds Yard and they climbed the fence just as Mickey had done the previous night. Instead of making for the boundary with the Simmonds Yard, Dan headed for the warehouse building. It was flat-roofed, and three stories high.

"We need somewhere we can see without being seen," explained Dan. "An observation post." He pointed upwards.

Jeff gulped. "Up there?"

"Up there," said Dan firmly. "Somehow we've got to get on to that roof."

They walked all round the warehouse, looking for a way up, and found it almost immediately. There was a rusty iron staircase bolted to the back of the building, presumably for a fire-escape. The trouble was it didn't come all the way down. It ended just above the ground floor.

Dan looked round. "Oildrums!" he said. "We'll build a platform."

Jeff groaned, but he knew it was no use arguing with Dan when he was in this mood. They rolled four empty oildrums beneath the ladder to make a platform and hoisted a fifth on top of them. By climbing onto this topmost oil-drum it was just possible to reach the lower rungs of the ladder.

Dan and Jeff climbed up onto the first lot of oil-drums and looked at each other. "I'll go first," said Dan. "It's my idea."

Jeff shook his head. "I'm heavier. If it'll hold me, it'll hold you too. You steady the drum."

Jeff clambered on to the top oil-drum, poised for a moment and jumped. He caught the ladder easily enough. It creaked alarmingly—but it held. He heaved himself up hand over hand, until he could get his feet on the rungs, and after that it was easy. He climbed steadily upwards until he reached the low stone parapet that ran round the top of the building. He climbed over, looked down, and waved encouragingly at Dan.

He saw Dan climb onto the oil-drum and leap gawkily, all arms and legs like a spider-monkey. Dan shot up the ladder at a terrific rate, clearly too nervous to stop moving, and a few minutes later he climbed panting over the parapet and collapsed on the roof beside Jeff. "Talk about easier said than done," he gasped. "You might have had the sense to talk me out of it!"

Recovering his breath, Dan looked round. They were on a flat square, tar-covered roof, baking hot in the morning sunshine. There was a trap-door in the centre of the roof. Jeff tried it, but it was bolted from below. He took off his shirt, rolled it up for a pillow, and stretched out appreciatively. "Very nice this. Bring up a few potted palms and it'd make a nice little roof garden!"

Dan nudged him in the ribs with a plimsolled foot. "Get up you idiot, we haven't come up here to sun-bathe. Come over to the other side—and keep down."

Crouching low they made their way to the other side of the roof and peered over the parapet. As Dan had hoped, they had a perfect aerial view of Simmonds Yard. They could see the whole of the yard itself with its heaps of old wrecked cars and rusting piles of scrap metal. They could see the wooden office, the big wooden gates in front of it, and the alleyway beyond them. The wooden gates were flung wide open now, and a big black dog was chained up just inside them. A man was standing at the open gates looking up the alleyway.

Dan took the binoculars from the haversack, and focused them on the man. As the distant figure sprang into sharp relief, Dan saw a stocky broad-shouldered man in a smart grey suit. He was smoking a cigarette in quick impatient puffs, and looking at his watch. "Harry Simmonds, I presume," said Dan. "Seems to be impatient about something."

Dan lowered the binoculars. "Right, we'll take it in turns. I'll go first and you can have lunch—and don't hog all the sandwiches." He raised the binoculars and Jeff started unpacking the food.

Dan had finished his watch and was eating his share of the sandwiches when Jeff said, "Someone coming." Dan jumped up to look.

A battered old lorry loaded with scrap metal came jolting down the alleyway, drove through the gates and stopped just in front of the hut. The driver got out and had a brief, and by the looks of it very unfriendly conversation with Harry Simmonds, who ended it by turning his back and going into the hut. The lorry driver climbed into the back of his lorry, chucked the scrap metal out at a furious rate, jumped back in the lorry and roared away.

After a few minutes, Harry Simmonds came out of the hut and took up his position at the gates. He looked at his watch, lit another cigarette and stood there waiting. The black dog yawned and stretched out.

Nothing happened for a while and Jeff said, "How long are we keeping this up then? I mean, it's not all that fascinating, is it?"

"Oh yes it is," said Dan softly. "We've picked a very good time—there's a crisis going on!"

"How do you make that out?"

"For a start, Harry Simmonds is in charge at the scrap yard—which isn't usual."

"More of your amazing deductions?"

"Look at the way he dresses, the way he picks his way through the muck. He's not at home here. I imagine brother Eddie usually takes care of the place."

"Guesswork," said Jeff sceptically.

"What about that scrap delivery just now? He didn't know where it was supposed to go. Wouldn't help unload it, either."

"All right then, where's brother Eddie?"

"Away on some kind of job. An important job. And I can tell you something else. Wherever he is, he's late getting back!"

The man in the grey suit was still pacing up and down by the gates. Through the binoculars Jeff saw him throw away a crumpled empty cigarette-packet, and fish out another.

A dusty blue Volkswagen van turned off the main

road and jolted down the alleyway. It drove through the gates and drew up outside the hut. A bulky figure climbed wearily out, Eddie Simmonds was back. His brother ran up to him and there was a long conversation, an angry one with a lot of arm waving. Several times the fat man turned and gestured angrily at the van. "Late back because he had a breakdown," whispered Dan. "His brother's very angry—but relieved to see him back." Suddenly the man in the grey suit stopped talking, turned—and stared towards the warehouse. Through the binoculars Dan saw Harry Simmonds point—and he was pointing straight at him. "Down," snapped Dan, and he pulled Jeff back down below the parapet.

"What's up?" hissed Jeff indignantly.

"You saw. They were looking straight at us!"

"Couldn't see much from down there, could they?"

Dan thought hard. "They could see the flash of sunlight on the binoculars. If they have just been up to something they'd be extra suspicious. Now they know someone's watching them." Dan started to gather up the remains of the lunch and pack them in the haversack making sure there was no trace left of their stay on the roof. He put the binoculars in the haversack, took a last look round, then gave a satisfied nod. "Okay, let's get moving."

Jeff looked over the parapet, then ducked down again. "We've left it a bit late. *They've* got moving before us."

Dan peered over the edge. The blue van was drawing up outside the warehouse fence. Fat Eddie jumped out, followed by his brother. Eddie put his shoulder to the wooden fence and smashed in a few palings. Both men squeezed through the gap.

Jeff started to climb the parapet, but Dan pulled him

back. "No good. They'll be waiting for us at the bottom."

"Well what if they are? What can they do?"

"Thump us for a start," said Dan. "And maybe worse."

"How do you mean—worse?"

"They could chuck us off this roof, wrench the ladder away, then go off and forget all about us. Tragic accident to kids playing on roof."

Jeff looked over the parapet again. The two men were standing by the oildrums now. Harry was pointing to the ladder, and Eddie was shaking his head vigorously.

"Don't think he fancies the climb," whispered Jeff. "Don't blame him either, not at his weight." He looked more cheerful. "Can't hurt us if they can't get up here, can they?"

"Maybe they can't. But while they're down there, we can't get down. We're trapped."

Liz looked at the tearful figure on the other side of the table. "Let me just see if I've got it straight. Sammy Price worked on one of the antique stalls in the market. He came in here every day and you eventually got very friendly."

"We were engaged," sniffed Shirley. "Look, he got me this ring off his stall." She held out her hand and showed an ornate ring—Liz reckoned it was worth about a pound.

Shirley looked like collapsing in tears again, and Liz hurried on. "Just over a week ago Sammy started acting strangely, is that right?"

"We wanted to get married, but Sammy was always broke. Then one particular morning he didn't come in

84

all day so I went round to his place in case he was ill."

"And was he?"

"Well, he *said* he was. But he wasn't in bed or anything. Just all pale and trembling, and he wouldn't go out all day. Or the next day come to that. I had to do all his shopping for him. He made me bring him all the papers to read."

Liz looked up sharply. "How long did all this go on then?"

"Right up to yesterday. He did start coming out a bit, but only after dark. He bought this silly cap and insisted on wearing it all the time. Miles too big it was, he looked like a walking mushroom."

"And last night he just disappeared?"

"He *said* he had an important business appointment earlier in the evening. He was supposed to come round to our house for supper later on. He didn't turn up, and he wasn't back when I went to his digs and when I went round this morning they said he hadn't been back all night...." Shirley really did collapse in tears this time, and Liz sat there thinking hard. Once she'd learned the missing boyfriend was red-headed, she'd been certain there was some connection with the case, and now she was more sure than ever. The sharp-faced girl came and patted her sobbing friend on the back. She looked accusingly at Liz. "You've upset her now, going over it all like that. Why are you so interested anyway?"

Liz jumped to her feet. "I'm sorry I can't explain properly, not just yet." She leaned over the sobbing girl. "Listen, Shirley, I don't think your boyfriend has just gone and left you. I think he may have been taken away. If he isn't back by tonight, I'd go to the police." Before they could ask any questions, Liz ran out of the cafe, and back up the hill.

When she got back to Rundles, there was no sign of Mickey. She hunted around and finally found him studying a toy shop window some way away. He started a hurried explanation about 'watching from a safe distance' but Liz wasn't interested. "Never mind Rundles, Mickey, we're finished with them. We're going to Simmonds Yard, to find the others."

Mickey was glad to be done with the boring shop watching and he followed Liz cheerfully down the hill. "What's all the panic?"

"If Dan and Jeff get spotted watching that yard, they could be in real danger. If my guess is right, we're not just dealing with robbery now. We're investigating a murder!"

10 Hunted

Dan peered over the parapet.

"They still down there?" whispered Jeff.

"The one in the suit is—the fat one seems to have disappeared."

Jeff was looking down at the trapdoor in the roof. "This must lead down into the building. If we could get it open...." They heaved at the trapdoor, but it was fastened firmly on the inside.

"Listen!" said Dan suddenly. He put his ear to the trapdoor, and Jeff did the same. They heard the sound of movement below them. It was coming closer...

"The fat one's in the building!" said Dan. "He's trying to find a way up. If he gets up to this trapdoor...."

"He'll never get it open," said Jeff uneasily.

"Oh won't he? The bolts will be on the inside, remember. Anyway, he can always smash it open. You saw the way he kicked that fence in."

Jeff felt the first stirring of panic. "What are we going to do?"

"Keep listening here. I'll see what's happening down below."

Dan peered over the edge. The man in the grey suit had lit another cigarette. He was just standing there, waiting.

Dan looked round for possible help, but they were too high up, and the warehouse was too isolated. There was a long-boat going along the canal, cars driving in the distance, people walking along the streets—but no-one near enough to hear a shout for help.

Dan looked over at Simmonds Yard, wishing miserably that he'd never heard of the place... and saw two very familiar figures hanging about at the end of the alleyway. Dan grabbed the binoculars. Sure enough, it was Mickey and Liz.

Liz peeped round the corner at the open wooden gates. "Place looks deserted. Maybe they've all gone off somewhere."

"Where are Dan and Jeff, then?"

"They might have gone in for a look round," said Liz slowly. "Or they might just be keeping an eye on the place."

"Why can't we see 'em then."

"They wouldn't want to be seen, would they? Or those villains might see them as well." Liz had an idea. "Dan took out some binoculars just before we left. He probably meant to keep an eye on the place from a safe distance. Somewhere up high probably." Liz looked round. "Top of that old warehouse would be the obvious place."

Mickey followed her gaze and said, "Hey, look!"

Liz looked... and saw a sudden gleam of light from the top of the warehouse. It came again ... and again. "It's a signal," said Liz. "Like a heliograph." She stared harder. There were long flashes and short ones—like dots and dashes.

"Come on Mickey," she yelled, "That's an SOS!"

Dan saw the distant figures wave and run off, and he went back to the trapdoor. "They got the message, I think."

Jeff kept his ear to the trapdoor. "What do you think they'll do?"

"Get the police if they've any sense . . . at least some-one knows we're up here now."

There came a muffled thumping from immediately below them . . . and the trapdoor shuddered under the impact of a heavy weight. Dan and Jeff looked wor-riedly at each other, not daring to speak. The trapdoor shuddered again, as someone shoved at it from below.

Dan jumped on to the trapdoor, and motioned to Jeff to do the same. Their combined weights should help to hold it down all right, he thought. The trap-door jolted again, and this time they could feel it move upwards a little.

Dan leaned close to Jeff and whispered, "If he does get through, tell him we were just playing soldiers. Say we told our parents where we were going."

The trapdoor jolted again. "You think he'll believe us?" said Jeff.

Dan shrugged, "It may make him think a bit. And listen Jeff, if he does try to . . . well, chuck us over, go for him with all you've got."

Dan's face was white with tension and his eyes were glittering. Jeff nodded and patted him on the shoulder. To himself he thought that the fat gorilla down below would swat them like flies. But Dan was right—all they could do was have a go.

They could hear hoarse breathing just below them now, like that of some great animal. Somehow the absence of shouts and threats made it all the more frightening. Their two opponents were working with calm efficiency. The fat man was coming up after them while the other waited calmly below. Just a little prob-lem that had to be tidied up.

A different sound came from below . . . a grinding and squeaking of metal. "Bolts must be rusted," whispered Dan. "Once he gets them open . . . "

Liz and Mickey ran round the corner of the warehouse fence and skidded to a halt. They saw the blue van, the broken fence the pile of oil-drums and the man waiting beside it. "They've got Jeff and Dan trapped up there," thought Liz. Somehow she knew she had only minutes to make a decision, and it had to be the right one. She grabbed Mickey's skinny arm. "Mickey, you stay here. Give me five minutes and then start on that bloke by the car. Chuck things, yell at him do what you like. You should be safe enough, he won't want to move from where he is. But if he does come after you, *don't get caught*."

Before Mickey could ask any questions, Liz turned and ran. Mickey turned and sprinted for the patch of waste ground. He ducked behind the cover of a bush and felt round for a nice big stone. . . .

The first stone whizzed over the fence and caught Harry Simmonds a nasty crack on the elbow. He yelled and spun round. Another stone crashed into the wall behind his head. The third missed, the fourth caught him on the knee. He gave a yell of pain, and ducked round the corner of the warehouse.

The trapdoor was bucking like a bronco now, with Dan and Jeff fighting to hold it down. Dan heard the noise from below and made a quick dash to the parapet to see what was going on. He saw the stocky man dodge round the side of the building followed by a hail of stones. A yell from Jeff brought him back to help with the trapdoor.

Mickey was just settling down to enjoy himself. He'd always been a good shot with any kind of missile and he was setting about the attack with scientific care. He couldn't throw straight at the target because the fence was in the way, so he developed a kind of lobbing technique, dropping the stones over the fence like mortar bombs. Suddenly Liz appeared behind him. "All right Mickey, that'll do."

To Mickey's astonishment Liz ran to the gap in the fence, standing in full view of the man he'd just been bombarding. "That your yard over there, Mister?" she yelled. "You'd better get back right away. Look!"

Liz pointed dramatically, and the man turned and looked. A column of thick black smoke was rising in the air over Simmonds Yard. Once she was sure he'd seen it, Liz ran back to Mickey. The stocky man froze for a moment, glared after Liz, made as if to chase her, then turned and ran for his van. Liz grabbed Mickey. "Shout for all you're worth." She ran back to the fence. "Dan, Jeff, come down. It's safe now. Come down quick!"

Mickey joined in the yelling. "Dan! Jeff!"

Up on the roof Dan heard the shouts. He ran to the edge and saw Liz and Mickey jumping up and down, yelling. There was no-one by the oil-drums and the blue van was driving away. "Come on Jeff," he yelled, and swung his legs over the parapet.

Jeff looked down at the trapdoor, which was rising a few inches now with each determined heave. Stepping back, Jeff jumped high in the air, and crashed down on the trapdoor with all his weight. There was a yell of pain from below. Jeff grinned in satisfaction, ran to the parapet, and started climbing down the ladder after Dan.

The didn't bother with the oil-drums going down, just hung at full length and dropped, first Dan then Jeff. Picking themselves up they sprinted to the gap in the fence where Mickey and Liz were waiting.

Fat Eddie gave a final angry heave. The hinges wrenched away from the wood, and he came through the trapdoor like King Kong, hands outstretched to grab his prey. He stopped, glaring round. The roof was empty.

He ran to the edge and looked over. His brother was gone. The car was gone. And two boys were just running out of the broken door in the fence, joining two others waiting on the other side.

"Come back here," roared Eddie stupidly. The smallest of the children paused, made an extremely rude gesture, and ran off after the others.

Tired, buised, grimy and hot, Fat Eddie stood on the sun-baked roof, swearing for all he was worth. He wiped the sweat from his eyes and turned to go back down the trapdoor. A patch of khaki caught his eye and he lumbered across to it. A canvas haversack was laying on the edge of the roof. He snatched it up in one huge paw and made for the hatch.

Harry Simmonds scorched down the alleyway and pulled up outside the gates to his yard. He'd half expected to find the place a raging inferno, but there was only the thick column of smoke, rising from behind the gate like an Indian smoke signal. He could hear the frantic howling of the dog.

He jumped out of the van, ran to the gates and dashed through. Inside he stopped a bleak smile on his face.

An old car tyre lay flat in front of the office door. Inside its circle someone had built a neat little bonfire of wood, paper and oily rags. An empty petrol can lay on its side close to the tyre. The dog, still on its chain, was barking furiously.

He went into the office and came out with a bucket

of water which he poured over the fire. It hissed and sputtered and finally went out.

He heard running footsteps and wheezing breath, and Fat Eddie came pounding through the gates. "Little baskets got away, didn't they?" he panted. "What you go chasing off for?"

"Thought the place was burning down, valuable property here, don't forget." He nodded to the rucksack in his brother's hand. "What you got there?"

Eddie tossed it over. "Found it on the roof."

Harry Simmonds stood turning the rucksack over in his hands. "Kids," he said softly. "One kid breaks in the yard last night. Two kids turn up on the roof, spying on us. Two kids turn up and help them get away—and one of them two was the little one from last night. A gang of kids, Eddie—and for some reason they're on to us."

"Suppose they go to the law?"

"Load of kids? Who's going to listen to them?"

Harry Simmonds looked through the rucksack, which held two empty coke cans, an empty sandwich bag, two apple cores and a battered old pair of binoculars without a case.

He was about to toss it aside when he glanced at the inside of the top flap. "Well, what do you know, Eddie? There's a name and address. Now we'll be able to return it to its owner."

Fat Eddie smiled. "Now?" he said eagerly. He took a canvas cosh from his pocket. Harry Simmonds shook his head. "No. Later tonight—when it's dark."

11 Dan alone

Back at Dan's house, the Irregulars held a celebration. They'd run most of the way without stopping, except for a quick call at the cake shop in the High Street. Dan made a pot of tea and they'd carried the tea things and the cakes to his room. Now everyone was eating, drinking and talking all at once.

Dan had told Liz and Mickey about what they'd seen from the warehouse roof, and Liz had told him about the girl who worked in the cafe.

Dan was marching up and down the room in excitement, tea in one hand, iced bun in the other. "It's like a jigsaw puzzle," he said. "We've got nearly all the bits now, and it's starting to fit together." He drained his tea mug and put it down, swallowed the last of his bun, and began counting on his fingers. "*One*—Sir Jasper decides to have his pictures cleaned. *Two*—he sends for Mr. Rundle, who spots a masterpiece amongst the junk, and tells his son Peter all about it."

Liz took up the story. "*Three*—Peter takes his girlfriend out to coffee and shows off about how clever his Dad is spotting the picture. Hanging about in the cafe is Sammy Price, who's *always* hanging about because one of the waitresses is his girlfriend. It's only a tiny place and he hears what Peter's saying."

"*Four*" said Dan, "Sammy is broke and needs money to get married. He knows Fat Eddie from somewhere and they decide to do the job together.

94

They pull it off but Sammy's terrified afterwards, and looks like giving the game away."

"*Five.*" squeaked Mickey excitedly. "They get him to go round their Yard—do him in! He's probably buried under a scrap pile somewhere. Or put in a car and squashed to a tiny cube, like that bloke in *Goldfinger.*"

Dan had made a different deduction. "It's possible, but I don't think they'd really commit murder so close to home. *But*—the fat one came back from a longish journey yesterday, he'd been away out in the country somewhere."

Jeff knew he was acting like Doctor Watson, but he just had to ask. "How did you work that out?"

"The amount of mud on the car. It was that thick grey-greenish kind you get on the Essex coast. I got a good look at it through the binoculars—" Dan stopped suddenly, mouth open. "I left them on the warehouse roof."

"Well it's not surprising is it?" said Jeff. "We left there pretty sharpish. I mean it's rotten luck losing your binoculars, but..."

"You don't understand," shouted Dan. "I left the haversack up there too."

"Well?"

"My name and address are written inside."

There was a moment's silence. Then Jeff gasped, "If that bloke who was after us found it..."

"He'd have to be blind to miss it," said Dan bitterly. "It was slap in the middle of a perfectly empty roof." He turned to the others. "Clear off the lot of you."

They all stared at him in amazement. Then Liz said, indignantly, "Look here, Dan Robinson, if you think we're just going to leave you..."

"Have some sense," said Dan. "I'm the only one

they know about, right? *So let's keep it that way*. If they find any of you here they could recognise you, follow you home. Then you and your families could be in danger. So beat it, quick. They could be on their way now."

It took quite a lot of persuading before they all agreed to go. It was Dan's final appeal that convinced them.

"They've seen *all* of us now at one time or another. If we stay in a group they'll spot us ten times as easily. I can dodge them on my own. And don't worry, I'm going straight to the police, I promise you."

They went off at last, Jeff the last to leave and the most reluctant to go. It was agreed they should all keep well away from Dan's house. Dan promised to telephone them and arrange a meeting when things looked safe, and he was sure he wasn't being followed.

Alone in the house, Dan went straight to the telephone, He fished the scrap of paper with Day's number out of his pocket, dialled, and asked for Detective-Constable Day. "Out of the station," said a bored voice at the other end. "Detective-Sergeant Summers here—can I help you?"

Dan remembered what Day had said about the Sergeant. Suddenly he couldn't face going through the whole unlikely story with some unbelieving stranger. "Never mind, I'll call later," he said, and put down the phone.

Dan sat thinking for a moment, then went to his typewriter and typed out a brief account of all his deductions, and of recent events. He addressed it to Detective-Constable Day at the local police station, wrote 'Police—Urgent' on the envelope, put a stamp on it and put it in his pocket, leaving the carbon in plain sight on his desk. If something did happen to him, he wanted someone to know who was to blame. Maybe the fact that the letter was in the post would be some protection in itself.

Just as he was about to leave the house, the phone rang. It was his mother calling from work. "Are you sure you'll be all right tonight?" she asked.

Dan stared at the phone. For a moment ot seemed as if somehow his mother knew what was happening. Then she said, "You do remember, tonight's my night for Gran?"

Once a week Dan's mother went to stay with *her* mother, who lived alone not far away. The old girl had been getting depressed since Dan's grandfather died, and this weekly visit was a way of cheering her up. When these nights coincided with Dan's father being away, it meant Dan spent the night in the house alone. He quite enjoyed it—usually.

For a moment Dan felt like asking his mother not to go, but he heard himself saying, "I'll be fine Mum, don't worry."

"I just wish your father wasn't away as well. Now, you *won't* sit up all night watching television, will you? And *do* remember, to pull out the plug when you go to bed. And get yourself a *proper* supper, not just cake and biscuits..."

She went on like this for some time with Dan saying, "Yes, Mum," and "Sure, Mum," and "I'll remember, Mum," at suitable intervals. Eventually she ran down, and Dan was able to say goodbye.

He felt both excited and scared as he put the phone down. His main worry had been that because of his carelessness with the haversack he would bring trouble to his family or his friends. Well, for the moment that danger was avoided. But there was still danger and from now on he was facing it on his own.

First thing to do was to get that letter posted. Dan had no patience with those detectives in stories who keep all their conclusions to themselves and then get killed or kidnapped before the information can do anyone any good. There was a postbox just on the other side of the road. He slipped on his denim jacket and went out. It was late afternoon by now, and people were starting to come home from work. Dan's house was in a fairly quiet side-street, and traffic was usually light. When he came opposite the pillar box, he waited till the road was clear and started to cross.

The way people act in traffic is based on the idea that the cars in the road are trying to miss you rather than hit you. Dan half-saw a vehicle turn the corner and hurried on a little, automatically assuming that the driver would slow down enough to allow him to reach the other side. There was a sudden roar of engine-noise, a blue shape hurtled towards him, and Dan leaped desperately for the pavement.

The wing of the speeding van caught him on the knee, and Dan rolled over and over on the pavement, thudding against the front-garden wall of the house opposite his own.

A shocked old lady helped him to his feet. "Terrible the way they drive these days, shouldn't be allowed..."

Dan's jeans were torn and he had a nasty-looking cut on his knee, but otherwise he was unhurt. A workman on a bike stopped at the kerb. "You all right, son? I tried to get the number for you, but there was mud all over the plates. It was a blue Volkswagen van though, I can tell you that."

"I'm fine, thanks, it's only a graze. I'll just go home and clean up." Dan picked up his letter which had fallen in the gutter, posted it, crossed the road again, and limped back to his house.

Reaction hit him as soon as he was back in the kitchen, and he found himself shaking uncontrollably. But a part of his mind was still calm and in control. "Shock!" he thought. He needed some hot sweet tea. Or was that out of date now? The hell with it, thought Dan, he'd have some anyway.

The tea made him feel better and soon the shaking stopped. He went to the bathroom, took off the torn jeans, bathed the cut on his leg and put a plaster on it. Then he went into his room and put on a clean pair of jeans. He found he was shivering in spite of the warm evening, so he pulled on a heavy sweater. Then he sat down in his armchair to think things out.

His first thought was to go straight to the police station. But he was still up against the problem of being a kid. He'd nearly been run over, fallen and scraped his knee? So what? They'd just assume he'd been careless in traffic. They'd ring his mother who'd come home in a panic, and there'd be no end of fuss and bother. Forget it, thought Dan.

He tried to put himself in his enemies' place. Instead of trying to be Sherlock Holmes, he had to think like the villainous Professor Moriarty. What would his enemies want? To kill him? Not really. Even hardened crooks didn't go round knocking people off quite so casually. They'd want to shut him up, though. They'd try to fake some kind of accident, so that he'd be lying in some hospital ward, out of their way. By the time he'd recovered, they would have sold the painting and they'd be safe.

Dan checked that the front and back door were locked, and wandered round the house wondering what to do next. Stay put till morning he decided. He called the police station twice more, but Day still wasn't back. He decided he ought to have supper, opened a tin of ravioli, but left most of it untouched. There was some ice cream in the fridge, but even that didn't tempt him. He tried to read but couldn't concentrate and he tried to watch telly, but found that the sounds and pictures were meaningless. Soon it got dark and after that the hours dragged slowly by. It was a *very* long evening.

Just before midnight he went down to the kitchen and started making cocoa. Suddenly the telephone rang. Probably Mum seeing if he was all right, thought Dan, though it was late for her to call. He picked up the phone and gave his number.

For a moment there was only heavy breathing on the other end of the line. Then a voice said, "Dan Robinson?"

"Yes?"

"You want to be more careful in traffic, sonny," wheezed the voice. "You could have a nasty accident.'"

The phone went dead.

12 Siege

Dan sat staring at the silent receiver, then put the phone down. His heart was pounding. He knew at once that the caller was Fat Eddie. Hearing his hoarse, wheezy voice made him feel as if the fat man was somehow in the house with him.

Really frightened now, Dan decided to go to the police station. He was just running down the stairs and was just about to open the front door when he suddenly stopped himself. Why had Eddie made the call? Just for the pleasure of scaring him? Hardly likely. They wanted him to go running out of the house in a panic. The police station was quite some way away, and somewhere on those dark streets they'd be waiting for him. Even if they didn't manage to run him over, a thump on the head from Eddie's cosh would do just as well. Kid out late on his own runs into anonymous mugger. Nothing to connect it with the Simmonds Brothers.

All right, so he wouldn't go out. He'd dial 999, they could send a police car round and take him to the station. As long as he was surrounded by nice large policemen they could laugh at him as much as they liked. He'd cheerfully spend the night in a cell if they wanted. Dan ran back to the sitting room and picked up the phone. The line was dead.

Since the wires ran down the side of the house, the enemy must be very close. Despite his panic Dan's mind was racing now working out problems and solutions like some berserk computer. If he simply refused to go out, what could they do then? Come in after him of course. Boy left alone in house runs into burglar, burglar hits boy on the head, pinches a few odds and ends, runs off in panic. Another nice anonymous crime.

Dan suddenly found he had too much to do to be frightened. The first thing was to check his defences. There had been one or two burglaries in Dan's neighbourhood recently, and Dan's father had been worried enough to have the house what he jokingly called burglar-proofed. There were good strong locks on both front and back doors, with supporting bolts and chains. There were even safety-locks on all the windows.

Dan reckoned the back door was the most likely point of attack. Anyone trying to break in the front would be in full view of the street, and although Dan's road was a fairly quiet one, people and cars went up and down until quite late at night. Presumably policemen went by too, though Dan couldn't remember ever having seen one.

He piled a barricade of chairs near the front door, and another near the back, just in case anyone did get through. What next? He needed a weapon. In most other countries there'd probably have been a gun in the house. Still in most other countries, the burglars would have guns too. Suddenly Dan remembered the golf-clubs. About a year ago, his father had decided he was putting on weight, and that he'd take up golf to help him keep fit. Unfortunately he'd been too busy to play more than once or twice and the largely-unused clubs were stuck in the cupboard under the stairs. Dan lugged out the dusty golf bag and pulled out the heaviest club he could find. Armed with this, he sat down on the stairs to wait.

Time crawled by. Dan began to wonder if he'd been dramatising things. Perhaps they'd rely on the near running over and the phone call to scare him off. Dan had just convinced himself of this reassuring theory and decided to go to bed when he heard a faint creaking sound from the back door. Then a sort of sharp crack. He got off the stairs and crept quietly along the corridor.

There were four panes of glass let into the upper part of the back door, forming a little window. Through them Dan could see a massive black shape blocking out the light from the night sky. There was a sharp crack, and a tinkle of broken glass. Eddie—surely it must be Eddie—had jabbed the glass from the lower-left hand pane, the one nearest the keyhole. A thick-gloved hand pulled the remaining fragments from the empty square. Then it reached through the gap and slid back the bolt on the door. It began groping around for the key.

Dan acted almost without thinking. He stepped forward and swung the club. It whistled through the air and caught the groping hand on the thumb.

There was a roar of agony, and the hand shot back through the gap. The bulky shape reeled off into the darkness.

Dan stood clutching the golf-club, his heart full of a fierce joy. That'd teach the fat slob to try and run *him* over. He raised the club again, ready to fight off any more attacks—and there came a sudden ring on the front doorbell.

Dan hesitated. Everything seemed quiet in the garden, and the back door was still solidly locked. He ran through the house to the front door and called, "Who is it?"

"Police, sir," said a reassuring voice. "Are you all

right? One of the neighbours reported an attempted break-in at the back."

Dan gasped with relief and started unbolting the door. No wonder the fat man had cleared off so quickly. One of the neighbours must have spotted him and given the alarm.

As he unlocked the door Dan called. "He tried to break in the back door—I think he's gone now."

"Just open up and let us through, sir," said the soothing voice. "We've got men round the back as well. He won't get away."

The last of Dan's dad's newly installed security devices was one of those chains that hooks across the inside of the door, so you can open it just a crack to see who's there, but still keep the door fastened. Dan opened the door, keeping the chain in place, and saw a raincoated man waiting on the step, a soft hat pulled over his face. Dan felt suddenly wary. The man's voice had been almost too policemanish—like someone doing a bad imitation of Dixon of Dock Green. And why was the man in plain clothes anyway? Surely ths police would have sent a car, not a CID man. And wasn't the caller rather short for a policeman? All these questions rushed into Dan's mind in seconds, and he left the chain where it was. "Would you mind showing me your warrant card please?" he said politely.

"Let me in and I'll show you with pleasure," said the voice. Dan wasn't having any. "You can push it through the gap," he said firmly. "I'm not opening this door till I see it."

A hand came through the gap all right, but it wasn't holding a warrant card. It wasn't holding anything. It grabbed Dan by the neck of his sweater, and dragged him towards the door. "Just open the front door sonny," said the voice. There was nothing policeman-like about it now.

Dan tried to pull away, but the hand held him fast—so he changed his tactics and shoulder-charged the door, slamming it shut on his attacker's wrist. There was a muffled cry. The hand let go its grip and drew back. Dan slammed the door shut, and barred and locked it again, leaning against it in relief.

A splintering crash came from just behind him.

He turned and ran back to the back door. It was shuddering beneath a series of ferocious kicks. Already he could see the wood splintering away from the lock. Fat Eddie had stopped bothering about unlocking the back door. He'd decided to kick it down instead!

Dan didn't even think of trying to fight him off with the golf-club. It would have been like facing a charging elephant with a pea-shooter. He shot up the stairs two at a time, heading for his room. There was a hatchway to the attic. If he could get up there...

As he ran a sudden inspiration came to him. It would take Fat Eddie another minute or two to get that back door open. Maybe there *was* still a way he could fight back.

Dan ran into the sitting room, put on the lights, pulled back the curtains and opened all the windows. He plugged in the telly, and switched it on. The midnight movie was still on—an old John Wayne war film. Dan turned the sound on full blast. He rushed to his father's stereophonic record deck, slapped on Beethoven's Ninth, and turned it up full volume. Just for good measure, he put Gary Glitter's *Greatest Hits* on his own record player and turned *that* up full as well. Finally he turned his mother's radio on full volume. By now the whole room was screaming with noise. Dan ran up to his room, slammed the door behind him, and wedged a chair against it.

Even up here, the din from the sitting room was shattering. It seemed to shake the floorboards. Keeping a wary eye on the door, Dan ran to the window and looked out. Lights were going on all down the street. Windows were being flung open as angry pyjama-clad figures shouted threats and reproaches into the night.

When they finally kicked down the door and ran upstairs the fat man and his brother ran into an almost solid wall of sound. John Wayne was bellowing that he'd hold this lousy foxhole to the very last Marine, and was mowing down rows of Japs with a very noisy machine-gun. Gary Glitter was howling at the top of his voice that he was the Leader of the Gang. Great chords of Beethoven's Ninth were rolling out into the night, and a BBC announcer was shrieking some very worrying news about the economy.

The two men were shaken and confused. A burglar wants darkness and silence, not a blaze of lights and a deafening pounding of music. This was breaking all the rules.

They actually ran into the sitting room and started switching things off, just to stop the unbearable din. As the noise lessened, the sound of angry voices could be heard from the street. And a car was drawing up outside the house.

The smaller of the two men ran to the window and looked out. A little crowd was gathering on the pavement and the car was a police car. The two men turned and ran. They crashed down the stairs, out the back door, and disappeared over the back garden.

Dan had been watching the scene in the street from his bedroom window with wholehearted enjoyment. The more angry neighbours came out of their houses, the better he was pleased. The arrival of the police car was the most welcome sight of all.

When two tall blue-clad figures jumped out and started hammering on his front door, Dan reckoned it was safe to come out of his room. He went downstairs to let them in, stopping on the way to switch off all his noisemakers. A blessed silence fell.

When he opened the front door two very large policemen stood looking curiously down at him. "Been having a bit of a party?" enquired the first one mildly.

Dan ushered them into the house and showed them the back door with the lock torn off. He explained he'd been alone in the house, heard someone breaking in, and had made as much noise as possible to frighten the burglar away.

"Why didn't you just dial 999?" demanded the second policeman. Dan said he'd tried, but the phone wasn't working. The policeman checked. It still wasn't. "Yes," said Dan, "he was perfectly all right, no he didn't want his mother told it would only worry her. No, he didn't want to go to a neighbour's house either, the burglars were scarcely likely to come back the same night."

The puzzled policemen wandered around the house taking notes and muttering to each other. Dan got the impression they wanted to arrest him, but couldn't decide what for. Eventually they took themselves off, telling him to be sure to come to the station next morning and make a statement.

Dan closed the front door after them, and locked and barred it. He shut the back door as best he could, and piled up a new barricade. He finished making his cocoa, carried it upstairs to his room and drank it and stretched out on the bed too tired to get undressed. As he drifted off to sleep he wondered if it was really safe and thought his attackers really weren't likely to try again that same night. They must be even more tired than he was.

When he opened his eyes to a blaze of sunshine next morning, he wondered if he'd been too optimistic. A man in a raincoat was standing by the bed looking down at him.

13 Counterattack

Dan jumped up in alarm, thinking the enemy had come back after all. Then he realised that this visitor was Detective-Constable Day. "Been having quite a time, haven't we?" said Day cheerfully. "Get yourself sorted out, and I'll see you downstairs. We'll have a working breakfast like the Prime Minister."

Dan scrambled to his feet, had a hasty wash, changed his shirt and went downstairs. Day was frying bacon and eggs in the kitchen. Dan put the kettle on and made a pot of tea and some toast.

As they started eating, Day took an envelope from his pocket and put it on the table. Dan recognised the letter he'd posted the night before. "First I get the memoirs of Sherlock Holmes in my morning mail. Then I hear of strange goings-on involving Daniel Robinson from the crime car boys. So I thought I'd pop round and study the scene of the crime."

Dan spread marmalade on his toast. "You'd better have the latest instalment," he said calmly. He told Day about the attempt to run him over and the later attack on the house. "Well that's it," he concluded. "What do you think?"

Day tapped the envelope. "About this? It all makes sense, all hangs together, could have happened just that way. And it's completely useless."

"You just said yourself, it makes sense," began Dan angrily.

Day pushed aside his plate and reached for his coffee.

"Time you learned a few of the facts of a copper's life, my son. Making sense has got nothing to do with it. It's not like in books. It isn't suspecting, it isn't even *knowing* whodunit that counts. It's proving it. We've got nothing here that would stand up in court. Nothing that would even *get* us to Court in the first place."

"You could search Simmonds Yard. I'm sure that painting's there somewhere."

"I'd never get a warrant. There's nothing to link the Simmonds brothers with the stolen painting."

"What about them trying to run me over?" said Dan indignantly.

"Who says it was them? Plenty of careless drivers about, and plenty of blue vans. Did you get the number? Got any witnesses?"

Dan sighed. The number plate of the van had been covered with mud, and he'd been too shaken to get the names of the old lady and the man on the bike.

"What about the break-in last night?"

"Not the first burglary in this area is it?"

"And the red haired man who's disappeared?"

"Probably just got fed up with his girlfriend and cleared off to dodge getting married."

Dan looked at him in despair. "And you believe all that?"

Day thumped the table, rattling the cups, and making Dan jump. "No! But it doesn't matter a monkey's cuss what I believe. I'm telling you what the Simmonds would say, what their lawyers would say in court—*if* we ever got 'em there, which I doubt."

"So what sort of evidence do you want?" asked Dan angrily. "A signed confession?"

"That'd do. A statement from this red-haired bloke for instance. He'd probably crack under a bit of pressure—that's why he's not around any more."

110

"Then why don't you start looking for him?"

"Oh we'll look *if* this girl of his reports him missing. But do you know how many people vanish in England every year? Just walk out, change their names and jobs. Disappearing is not a crime, not in itself."

Dan was thinking hard. He was sure his reconstruction of what happened was true. And if it was true, there must be some way to prove it. "What about Fat Eddie. He's got a record, hasn't he? Couldn't you pull him in for questioning?"

"Going straight now isn't he? Paid his debt to society. There'd be howls of police persecution if we did that. Besides, do you think Sir Jasper could pick him out on an identity parade?"

Dan shook his head. "I doubt it."

Day finished his tea. "You see what we're up against? In this country, the thieves and villains have got their legal rights just the same as you and me. Fair enough, that's the way it ought to be. But a clever villain knows how to use those rights to protect himself. Come to that you couldn't even say Harry Simmonds was a villain. Not his fault if his brother's a bad lot. Harry's always stood by him, tried to get him to go straight. And Harry himself has got a spotless record. Prominent local business man, gives money to good causes." Day grinned ruefully. "He's even got a licence for a shotgun—and you have to be next to a saint to get a gun licence in this country."

Dan nodded absent-mindedly, his mind still on the case. "So, you need a statement from one of those involved or some solid evidence linking the Simmonds with the crime—like their being found with the missing painting in their possession?"

Day nodded.

"All right, I'll see what I can do for you!"

111

"You will not," said Detective-Constable Day severely. He picked up Dan's report. "I don't deny you've done a pretty impressive job here, and I reckon there's every chance you're on to something. I'll pass the information on, and if we can we'll act on it. *We'll* keep an eye on Simmonds Yard, but you and your mates keep away from there. I want your promise on that."

Dan nodded reluctantly. "Okay, okay. But suppose they come after me again?"

Day said grimly. "I reckon they'll call it quits after last night. Just to make sure, I'm going to try bluffing them. I can probably throw enough of a scare into them to make them leave you alone—but you've got to leave them alone. Keep on sticking your head in the lion's den, and someone will bite it off."

Dan had a busy morning after Day had gone. He went to the house of old Miss Parsons next door, apologised for all the fuss last night, and begged the use of her phone. He called the GPO to get his own phone repaired, his mother at work in case she was worried (saying nothing about the break-in) and the local hardware shop for a man to repair the back-door. Last of all he called the rest of the Irregulars to tell them it was safe to come round.

Jeff, Liz and Mickey all arrived at his house in quick succession and listened in amazement to the story of his night's adventures. Mickey just didn't believe him until Dan showed the broken back door and his cut knee as evidence. Then he said enviously, "Some people have all the luck!"

Dan finished his story over coca-cola and biscuits in the kitchen, and when it was over Jeff said firmly. "Well, that settles it. We leave it to the police from now on."

Liz sighed. "It does seem a shame, though. Talk about so near and yet so far..."

"That's right," said Mickey. "A bit more detecting and we'd have got 'em. Don't suppose the police will ever do it. I bet that copper doesn't even pass the information on."

Detective Constable Day was wrestling with his conscience about Dan's "dossier" at this very moment. He was pretty sure the boy *was* on to something. Why else should the Simmonds have reacted to his enquiries so violently? But how could he approach Detective-Sergeant Summers with a load of theories run up by some kids as a kind of holiday project? He could just imagine the blast of withering sarcasm he'd get. Summers' childhood was long behind him, and he had no liking or sympathy for kids. One thing *he* could do, thought Day, was put a bit of a scare into the Simmonds Brothers. He called the Yard and a polite voice said, "Simmonds Scrap Metals. Can I help you?"

"Mr. Harry Simmonds?"

"That's right."

"Detective-Constable Day, sir. Local CID."

There was a silence at the other end of the phone. Then the voice said calmly. "Dear, oh dear. I hope that brother of mine hasn't been getting in trouble?"

"Not as far as I know, sir. I was calling about some children."

Another silence. Then "Children?"

"That's right, sir. Kids. I understand you've been having trouble with them."

There was an even longer silence. Day could almost hear Harry Simmonds thinking, wondering if Dan had made an official complaint, preparing his denials. "What do you mean exactly," said the voice politely.

Day smiled to himself, but kept his voice formal. "I understand you've been having trouble with them, sir. Trespassing on your property, lighting fires and that sort of thing."

This time the silence was an astonished one. Then Simmonds said, "We did chase a few off recently. They were playing about in the empty warehouse next door, and I was afraid they'd hurt themselves. Nothing very serious though."

Deliberately Day hardened his voice. "It could get *very* serious though sir—if someone got hurt. I happen to know the children concerned. In fact, I've had quite a long chat with one of them. I think I can promise they won't bother you again. I suggest you just let the matter drop, sir."

"I see," said the voice thoughtfully. "I'm sure you're right, Officer. If they stay away from the yard, they won't come to any harm, will they? Thank you for calling."

Day smiled grimly to himself. On the surface, a friendly chat between a local businessman and a friendly policeman. But he was pretty sure Harry Simmonds had read between the lines. If anything now happened to Dan, or to any of his friends, the Simmonds would be asked some very awkward questions.

Harry Simmonds sat staring at the phone. Then he went to the door of the hut and yelled "Eddie!"

Fat Eddie Simmonds came lumbering in from the yard and listened bemusedly while Harry told him of Day's call.

"Perishing kids," he rumbled. "I'll—"

"You'll nothing," snarled Harry. He brooded for a moment. "But I think I'd better go down for a day's

114

shooting. Just in case that copper knows more than he's letting on. Can't take any chances now. The Sheik's coughing up tomorrow."

He went to the steel cabinet and opened it to reveal his shooting clothes—waterproof trousers, an anorak, an old pair of waders. Propped in the corner was a double-barrelled shotgun. Harry took it out and polished it with a scrap of oily rag. "Nasty, dangerous mud down on that coast," he said conversationally. "Anyone fell into one of those soft patches he'd probably never be found."

Not for the first time, Fat Eddie shuddered at his brother's coldness. "Poor old Sammy, he's not a bad little bloke." Then he cheered up. "Still, better to split between two than between three..."

In Dan's kitchen the argument was still raging. "I tell you it's just not worth it." Jeff was saying. "If we keep on with this, we're going to end up run over, or coshed or something. It's not safe to go on."

"It may not be safe to stop either," said Liz unexpectedly. "As long as they know we suspect them we're still in danger. Suppose they're not scared off by this policeman?"

"We'll end up getting blasted with buckshot," said Dan gloomily.

"Buckshot?" asked Liz. "They don't carry guns, surely."

"Well according to Day, Harry Simmonds has got a shotgun..."

Dan's eyes widened. Suddenly his brain started racing again, leaping from conclusion to conclusion almost of its own accord. "And why has he got a shotgun eh? So he can go shooting—wildfowl, things like that. And where do people go shooting? Nice

115

isolated places in the country, like the Essex marshes. There was Essex mud on the van. And where would you send a nervous friend who needed a bit of peace and quiet?"

"Sammy Price," breathed Liz. "You mean they've stowed him away somewhere, so he can't talk?"

"Well it's possible, isn't it?" said Dan. "If Harry Simmonds *has* got some kind of base out in the country, a cottage or even a caravan, it would be the obvious place..."

"They'll have done him in," said Mickey, with gruesome relish. "Maybe we can find the lonely, nameless grave."

Jeff shook his head. "I still don't think they'd risk murder. But hiding him would make very good sense."

"But *where?*" said Dan. He reached for the phone, remembered it wasn't working, said "Hang on a bit, everybody," and popped next door again.

Detective Constable Day was still wondering how he was going to put Dan's theories to his superiors, when the telephone rang, and he heard Dan on the line. "You know you said Harry Simmonds had a shotgun licence? Where does he do his shooting?"

"No idea. I suppose it might be in the files somewhere."

"Could you look it up—please? It could be really important."

"All right," said Day reluctantly. "Hang on."

He went to a filing cabinet, and rooted through it until he found what he was looking for. "Here you are, here's his letter of application. 'I have rented a rough shoot on Oyster Creek Island in Essex and therefore wish to apply'... quite the landed gent our Harry."

"Thanks a lot," said Dan excitedly. "That's marvellous. Just what I wanted."

A little belatedly, it occurred to Day to ask why Dan needed the information. "Here, you're not going to..."

"Thanks again," said Dan, and the phone went dead.

Dan dashed back into his own house and said briskly, "Get yourselves organised you lot, we're off for a day in the country." After a lot of searching they found Oyster Creek Island on one of Dan's father's big Ordnance Survey maps. It was a tiny island on an Essex river estuary. "Liverpool Street, I think," said Dan. "Can't take more than a couple of hours. Let's get moving!"

"You mean *now?*" said Jeff resignedly. He already knew the answer. There was no chance of stopping Dan once he got going.

"*Now,*" said Dan firmly. "We'll have to have a whip round for the fares, day returns will do. I can get something out of the Post Office. We'd better pack some food and drink, make a proper picnic of it. The island's probably somewhere pretty isolated."

Everything seemed to go in a whirl. They all rushed round to Jeff's house, cadged sandwiches, fruit and cake off his mum, and used her phone to call Mickey's and Liz's mums to get permission for the trip. Before long they were all on the Underground, heading for Liverpool Street station. When they arrived Liz who'd been appointed treasurer bought four half-fare day returns to the coast and soon they were all sitting in a Southend train, packed in with Mums, Dads, and children on their way to the seaside. It was a terrible squash, but everybody seemed cheerful, and the four children found themselves forgetting the grim purpose of the trip, caught up in the holiday atmosphere.

"Have to change," said Dan wrestling with the map. "We'll probably go on one of those little local diesels."

They reached a busy little market town and here they changed to a kind of toy train, only three carriages long. This train was crowded too, this time with local farmers' wives returning from a morning's shopping. The little train chugged through flat green fields, stopping at a succession of tiny country stations. Soon there was the gleam of water on their right, and then they saw white sails moving through the fields, as though the yachts were sailing on land.

They all piled excitedly off at their destination and walked down to the waterfront. Mickey gasped in astonishment at the rows and rows of yachts moored in the wide estuary. "It's a floating traffic jam" he said.

Dan looked at the map again. "All we do now is follow the river upstream and we'll come to the island somewhere on our left. Get moving you lot, time's getting on."

As they walked along the embankment, the road became narrower and narrower till it turned into a footpath, the pubs and cafes and houses fewer and fewer. Eventually they were walking along a rough track on top of the low sea-wall, river on their left, and flat green fields on their right. The sun was shining, a breeze ruffled the river, and white-sailed yachts floated silently by. It was hard to imagine any connection between a place like this and the sinister Simmonds brothers and their gloomy Yard. Let alone a missing witness, and a stolen masterpiece back in London.

At last they came to a long, thin oval-shaped island huddled close to the bank of the river. There were notices stuck on posts along its banks. "Keep Out", "Private" and, most sinister of all, a crudely daubed skull-and-crossbones with the single word "Danger!" They had found Oyster Creek Island.

Opposite the island was a gap in the sea wall. A narrow country lane ran at right angles to the river, and down through the gap, and disappeared into the river. There were one or two dilapidated looking boats moored on the muddy bank, and that was all. There was no sign of life.

Liz gazed across the narrow stretch of river to the sinister-looking island. "Well, there it is! What do we do now?"

14 Showdown

It was Jeff, practical as ever, who took charge. He pointed to one of the rowing-boats moored on the bank. "We borrow one of those and row across."

"No oars or rowlocks," objected Liz.

"Simple. We paddle with a floorboard."

Dan smiled to himself. All this was typical of old Jeff. Always reluctant to get started, always refusing to give up once he'd got going.

Suddenly Mickey said, "I can hear a car coming down that lane."

"As long as it's not an old blue van," said Liz uneasily.

"Well, it could be," said Dan. "Let's all get down—just in case." They all scrambled into the overgrown ditch that ran along the landward side of the sea wall. They heard the car draw up at the end of the lane, and someone get out. They heard the door slam, a muffled bark and then a strange rhythmic wheezing sound. Then there came the sound of something being dragged away from them.

After what seemed a safe interval, they all looked out of the ditch. It was a blue Volkswagen van, parked very close to where they'd been hiding. They climbed the sea wall and peered over the top. A stocky figure in waders and anorak was dragging a rubber-dinghy towards the water.

Dan realised that the wheezing sound must have been the sound of the dinghy being pumped up. Then he realised something else, The figure was dragging the rubber-dinghy with one hand. Its other hand held a shot-gun.

They saw the man launch the dinghy, jump in and paddle towards the island.

When he reached the other side he beached the dinghy, squelched along the muddy shore and disappeared from sight.

Jeff looked at Dan. "That was Harry Simmonds wasn't it?"

Dan nodded. "Well, at least we know this is the right place. I wonder why he's come down here today?"

"We'd better get after him and find out," said Jeff. He turned to Liz and Mickey. "Now listen you two, no arguments. It's dangerous enough for two, but it'll be impossible for four. And we need you two on shore, to guard the rear." Mickey and Liz nodded without speaking. Things were too serious now for the usual grumbles.

Jeff and Dan ran down the water, untied the most seaworthy dinghy. To their delight they found a single oar laying in the bottom.

They shoved the dinghy off and jumped in, Jeff paddling gondolier fashion with the oar, Dan helping with a loose floorboard. In no time at all they had crossed the narrow stretch of water and were stuck in the mud on the other side. They climbed out of the dinghy and squelched onto firmer ground.

Once they were actually on the island they realized it had a big dip in the centre and a high rim around the edge. Nothing in the centre of the island could be seen from shore. It was an ideal hiding place. Muddy tracks led away from the dinghy, and Jeff and Dan followed them. The island was a mixture of mud, seaweed and the same rough grass that grew on the sea-wall. The track led them clear across the island to a battered old houseboat moored in a narrow creek on the far side. It was little more than a box-shaped super-structure built up on a pontoon hull and its once-white paint was shabby and peeling. They could hear a voice coming faintly from inside the boat. They dropped down and crawled across the tufted grass till they could hear what it was saying.

When they were close enough, Dan recognised the calm, level tones of Harry Simmonds. "Look, Sammy," he was saying, "It's nothing personal. Only things have changed now. These kids have been poking around and the law's taking an interest. It's a tricky time—we've found a buyer, and we can't risk him being scared off. So, all in all, we decided it would be safer if you weren't around any more."

There came a kind of incoherent babbling from inside the boat, but Harry's calm voice cut across it. "I know you wouldn't *mean* to talk Sammy, but I don't think you'd be able to stand a going-over from the law. It's better this way, it really is . . ."

Dan could hardly believe what he was hearing. Harry Simmonds was about to commit a ruthless murder. The worst thing of all was that his own investigations were responsible. Dan wriggled closer until he could see over the stern of the boat. Harry Simmonds stood balanced on the little deck. He was aiming the shot-gun inside the cabin and beyond him Dan could just see a huddled figure cowering on a bunk. Dan acted almost without thinking. He jumped up, ran forward and went flying through the air in one tremendous leap. He landed on the deck of the houseboat with a thud, crashing into Harry Simmonds just as he pulled the trigger. One barrel of the gun went off with a crash and shattered one of the houseboat portholes.

From the bank Jeff saw Dan grappling with Harry Simmonds and jumped on board to help. Harry Simmonds wasn't as big as his brother but he seemed almost as strong and it was soon clear he was more than a match for both of them. Dodging a vicious kick Dan heard Jeff grunt, *"Get him overboard."* Grabbing a leg each they lifted and heaved, pitching the man right off the deck of the houseboat. He landed in the river with a tremendous splash. Gasping, Dan and Jeff looked inside the houseboat. A skinny, redheaded man in shabby clothes was huddled sobbing on a bunk. They lugged him out and Dan helped him off the boat and onto the bank. Jeff snatched up the shot-gun, and looked over the other side of the boat. Harry Simmonds, waist-deep in water was wading towards them.

Jeff jumped from the boat and dragging their shuddering companion between them, the two friends ran back across the island. They practically threw the little man into the rowing-boat and ran waist-deep into the water to shove it off. Before he jumped in, Jeff aimed the shot-gun at the nearby rubber dinghy and fired the second barrel. There was a bang and a hiss of air and the dinghy began to collapse.

Jeff jumped in the rowing-boat, grabbed the oar from Dan, and they began paddling back to the other side. Just as they reached it, they heard a bellow of rage from the island. Harry Simmonds was lurching towards his ruined dinghy. He was covered in dripping black mud, and looked, as Dan said later, very much like the Creature from the Black Lagoon.

As they ran towards the sea-wall. Dan heard the roar of an engine. To his astonishment he saw that Liz was behind the wheel of the blue van, Mickey beside her. Somehow, Dan, Jeff and the rescued Sammy all squeezed into the big front seat with them, and the van roared off.

A furious barking could be heard coming from the back.

Liz had been practising on her mother's car on quiet country roads for some time, waiting till she was old enough to take the test. She drove as quick as she dared up the narrow winding lane that led away from the hard.

"Didn't know you could drive," shouted Jeff as they jolted up the lane.

"He'd left the keys in," said Liz coolly. "I heard the shots and thought you might need a quick getaway!"

They drove along the narrow rutted lane until they came to a barrier—a pair of level crossing gates stretched across the lane. A railway-line cut across the lane, and on the other side of the track was one of the tiny stations they'd passed through on the way down. Dan jumped out and tried the gates but they were locked. He looked along the track and saw that the signal was up. He went back to the others. "I think there's a London train due." he said. "We can't take this van much further, anyway. The police might suspect Liz hasn't got a licence!"

They all got out of the van and before anyone could stop him Mickey opened the back door. The enormous black dog they'd seen at the yard jumped out and sat down, looking at them with intelligent interest.

"What are we going to do with him?" asked Liz.

Unafraid, Mickey patted the dog's head and its tail thumped the ground. "Well we can't leave him, can we He'll just have to come with us!"

They crossed the tracks and a few minutes later the little diesel appeared. They all piled in, four muddy children, a frightened man and a big black dog.

The red-headed man seemed in a daze, unable to realise that he had been rescued. Dan smiled reasssuringly at him and said, "Sammy Price, I presume? The well-known art thief?"

The little man stared. "Who *are* you kids? How do you know so much about me?"

Liz said, "Your girlfriend's been very worried about you, Mr. Price. It's time you came back to London to see her."

Suddenly the little man seemed to realise what had so nearly happened to him. "He was going to shoot me," he said indignantly. "Me!" He said it as though things wouldn't have been nearly so bad if the attempted murder had involved someone else. "He was actually going to murder me and bury me in the mud!"

"That's right," said Dan cheerfully. "We saved your life. Now don't you think you'd better tell us all about the robbery? How did you first meet the Simmonds brothers?"

Sammy Price started talking as if someone had taken a stopper out. "I used to buy stuff off them for my stall. Pewter pots, copper, stuff like that. When I heard this bloke in the cafe going on about the painting, I got the idea of stealing it. Eddie Simmonds was the only villain I knew . . . "

Harry Simmonds drove like a maniac all the way back to London. Thanks to the ebbing tide he had been able to wade across the shallow creek, though the water had been waist deep. He'd had a long wet tramp up the lane to find his van. Now he was desperately trying to get back to London before the children—and Sammy Price. It was a long weary drive through the suburbs and across most of London. He stopped several times to try and telephone his brother but the first two boxes he tried had been vandalised and when he finally found one that worked there was no reply at the other end.

Everything seemed normal when at last he drove up the alleyway to his Yard. It was just getting dark and he could see Eddie sat drinking tea in the office hut. Perhaps he was in time after all.

He parked the van, jumped out, and ran into the hut. "Eddie, he got away. Those lousy kids turned up again. We've got ta..."

He broke off as a sharp-featured young man in a raincoat stepped from behind the door of the hut. "I'm afraid Eddie isn't going anywhere, Mr. Simmonds. He's under arrest—so are you, incidentally."

Harry Simmonds turned to run. A police car roared down the alley blocking his escape. All at once the hut seemed full of policemen. Four kids turned up out of nowhere, the smallest holding a big, black dog—his dog—by the collar. "Get 'em Killer," roared Simmonds, desperate for some small revenge.

The littlest kid said quietly. 'Down boy,' and the dog obediently sat down, wagging its tail.

Harry Simmonds shook his head bewildered. Everything had gone so wrong so fast...

Detective-Constable Day said, "We've got the full story from Sammy Price, Mr. Simmonds. Somehow he lost all sense of loyalty once you tried to kill him. When your brother found out that Sammy had talked, he talked as well. Told us how *you'd* planned the whole thing. In fact there's really only one thing he hasn't told us—the whereabouts of the missing painting itself."

Harry Simmonds scowled and said nothing. Dan said, "I think I can tell you that. It's suddenly occurred to me—I don't really see these two as birdwatchers." He stepped forward and tore down the poster of

British birds. Tacked to the wall behind it, was a faded painting of a group of tumbled stones—the Constable 'Stonehenge'.

That was the end of it all—or very nearly. Sammy Price confessed the story of the robbery to practically every-one in sight and got off with a fairly light sentence. The Simmonds brothers took it in turns to accuse each other not only of this crime but of many others. It emerged that Harry Simmonds had always been the brain behind his fat brother's crimes, taking most of the profits and keeping his own reputation spot-less—while Eddie was the one who went to prison when things went wrong. Eventually *both* got sent to prison for a very long time, though of course this didn't happen until some time later.

More immediately, Liz's mother sold the story of the Baker Street Irregulars to the local press. They all got their photographs in the papers, posing with a delighted Sir Jasper beside the restored picture. Not that the picture was restored for very long. Mr. Rundle whipped it off to his burglar-proof vaults, and it was later sold at Sotheby's for enough to keep Park House going for quite some time.

The holidays ended, they all went back to school and a very subdued Webb presented Dan Robinson with a copy of *The Hound of the Baskervilles*. Dan was quite surprised at this. By now he'd forgotten how the whole thing started. . . .

One final thing. When both Simmonds brothers were arrested there was no-one left to look after the big black dog called 'Killer'. They'd bought the dog cheap, obviously as stolen property. The original owners couldn't be traced and eventually the poor dog ended up in Battersea Dogs' Home. Mickey put in a claim, but his mum wouldn't hear of it—they had a dog and two cats already. For a time it seemed the dog might have to be destroyed. Mickey went round to Dan almost in tears, and Dan remembered that, after she'd finally learned about the attempted break-in, his mother had had mild hysterics and talked about getting some kind of watchdog. So he took her at her word and brought Killer home with him. Dan's mum said she hadn't really meant a dog as big as a horse—but she didn't go back on her word. Dan christened the dog Baskerville. As Jeff said, when he heard, "What else?"

Which explains why, when Dan's dad finally got back from his business trip, arriving unexpectedly in the middle of the night because of plane trouble, he ended up with what felt like a ton of black dog pinning him to the front doormat, and shaking the whole house with deafening woofs.

Dan came downstairs in his pyjamas, called off the dog and said sleepily, "Oh hullo Dad, you're back. Quite a lot's happened while you've been away...'